# A MATCH MADE IN IRELAND

ESCAPE TO IRELAND SERIES BOOK 1

MICHELE BROUDER

This is a work of fiction. Names, characters, places and incidents are either a product of the author's imagination or are used fictitiously, and any resemblance to actual persons, living or dead, events, or locales is entirely coincidental.

Editing by Jessica Peirce

Book Cover Design and Formatting by www.madcatdesigns.net

A Match Made in Ireland



*To God be the Glory.*

*For Mike,*
*Always, always, always.*

# CHAPTER ONE

Nothing was going to ruin Ruth Davenport's night tonight. Not even her leg. It was a good omen that it didn't ache. If she could whistle, she would, and if her limbs were more reliable, she'd skip and hop up and click her heels together in a Julie Andrews, *Sound of Music* kind of way.

Her phone pinged with a new text, and when her editor's name appeared across the screen, Ruth rubbed her bottom lip with her finger. She was supposed to be working on her next book, and her editor wanted an idea what it was about. The only problem was that Ruth didn't know what it was about. Yet.

She tossed her phone into her purse, grabbed

her lavender cardigan, and shrugged it on over her knee-length, sleeveless floral dress. Glancing in the mirror on the way out, she nodded in approval at the look of her red hair, with the sides clipped back.

The late spring evening was warm, and a smile crossed her face as she strolled along South Street toward the Mill Street pub, the neighborhood bar slash microbrewery where she hung out with her sister and friends.

As fast as her legs could take her, she made her way toward the pub, humming the tune of a love song from one of the many romcoms she liked to watch. Most of the bars and restaurants in this area were recent. There was a time when she wouldn't have been caught dead in this part of town.

Arriving at the pub, she checked her reflection in the front window. She rubbed her damp palms on her dress and drew in a deep breath before pushing open the door of the bar. Raised voices and music from the jukebox spilled out, and the smell of popcorn made her stomach growl.

Tonight was the night. After three months of crushing on Steve Acola, she was going to ask him out. It had taken her two weeks to get to this point.

Months ago, she and Steve had been randomly assigned as teammates in a dart tournament. He had been solicitous and engaging. After that, whenever they'd run into each other at the bar they'd share a drink and a few laughs, and she found herself frequenting the place more often than usual with the hopeful expectation of running into him.

He reminded her so much of the heroes she had written. And with five romance books under her belt, she knew a hero when she saw one. Clean-shaven and tall, with blond hair and blue eyes, he was exactly the kind of leading man she liked to write about. Dream about.

After giving it serious consideration, she'd decided she'd ask him out to dinner. She'd convinced herself that he must have a little bit of interest in her, as well. Maybe he was shy, and just needed a slight push. Ruth was more than willing to give him a gentle shove in the right direction.

As she scanned the crowd for any sign of him, she smiled and waved at the familiar faces who greeted her. Thursday nights was the dart league and a special on the tacos, and it was two deep at the bar. She tried to squeeze through to order a drink, but the man in front of her stepped back without looking and landed a sharp elbow to her breast. Her smile was quickly replaced with a grimace. By morning there was sure to be a bruise. The stranger turned around and raised his eyebrows. "Uh, sorry."

He moved along, and Ruth pushed her way into the vacated space, lifting her purse and placing it on the bar. When Johnny, the bartender, eyed her, he nodded and asked, "The usual?"

She nodded, and he pulled a glass from underneath the bar and filled it simultaneously with tonic water and a shot of vodka. He topped it off with a slice of lemon and slid it across the bar. She laid a twenty down and waited for her change, then tipped him and threw her wallet back into her purse.

Her mouth dry, she took a quick sip of her drink as she scanned the room, looking for an empty table. The faces in the crowd were familiar; like her, they were regulars. But this was her first time going to a bar alone. Her stomach growled, and she rolled her eyes. How could she possibly be hungry? Earlier, she'd eaten two servings of a roast beef dinner.

Out of the corner of her eye, she caught sight of a couple standing up to leave a table over by the popcorn machine. *Perfect.* She hurried over and laid her drink on the high table, claiming it. It was far enough away from the speakers so she wouldn't have to shout, and with a great view of the entrance, she could watch who came in. Namely Steve. His pattern was Thursday and Friday nights after nine. Hopefully, he'd stay true to form tonight.

A baseball game played on the big-screen TV,

and normally Ruth would watch it, but she couldn't take her eyes off the door, almost willing Steve to appear as if by magic. She didn't have to wait long to be rewarded. As her heart rate picked up, her courage faltered.

The object of her affection had walked in, greeting people he recognized. There wasn't a hair out of place or a wrinkle in his shirt.

When he saw her, his eyes widened and he broke into a smile. Ruth melted, delighted to have caused that reaction in someone. She was further encouraged when he made his way through the crowd toward her.

"Hi, Ruth, how are you?" he asked.

Nodding and smiling, she leaned forward, elbows on the table. "I'm well, thank you."

"Can I get you another drink?" he asked, nodding toward her nearly empty glass.

"Yes, please. A vodka and tonic," she said.

He pointed his finger at her. "With lemon, not lime, right?"

She reddened, secretly pleased that he remembered this little detail about her.

As he headed toward the bar to get a round of drinks, she practiced asking him out in her mind.

Soon he returned, setting the drink on the table

in front of her. He took a long swig from his beer bottle.

"How've you been?" he asked.

She nodded quickly. "Good? How's work?" she asked.

He was a physical therapist, and he loved his job. And she loved hearing about it. *See?* she thought. They were a perfect match.

He went into detail about his work at a rehab center on the other side of town. He leaned into her and made a joke, and Ruth felt her pulse quicken. As unobtrusively as possible, she studied him: the animated expression, the blue eyes, the immaculate sandy-blond hair.

"How's your leg?" he asked. "Will the warmer weather and increased humidity affect it?"

The first time he had asked her about her limp, months ago now, she'd been embarrassed to have attention called to it, but he had been kind, even asking her permission to question her about it.

She shook her head. "No, not anymore. It's mainly stress that aggravates it."

He nodded, seemingly unfazed by it. *He might just be a keeper*, she thought.

There was a lull in their conversation. Ruth drew in a deep breath and decided that this was as good a time as any. Her mouth had gone dry again. She took a gulp of her drink.

"Steve, there's something I want to ask you," she started.

He looked at her expectantly and smiled. "Actually, there's something I want to ask you, as well."

"Really?" she asked. She became dizzy and jittery. *Calm down.*

A sudden shift in the atmosphere of the pub caused Steve to look over his shoulder. It was a shift Ruth was quite familiar with.

Nicole.

Looking up, she saw her younger sister standing in the doorway, confirming her suspicion. Voices quieted down and heads turned when Nicole entered a room. It had been that way for as long as Ruth could remember.

Nicole had been blessed with the kind of beauty you saw on billboards and glossy magazine covers. Everyone, not just men but women and people of all ages, stopped and stared. She was also the life of the party, which added an exponential component to the overall package. Nicole caught sight of them and headed their way. Along the way, she greeted people, not with a wave but with a hug and a kiss.

Steve turned back and whispered, "Ruth, I was wondering…"

Ruth looked up at him in anticipation.

"I was wondering if you could put in a good word for me with your sister," he said.

Ruth's mind went blank. She blinked. "Excuse me?" she asked, her face reddening. Everything shrunk inside her and she felt as if her heart constricted.

Steve looked over toward Nicole and nodded. "Your sister. I think she's beautiful. Do you think she'd be interested in someone like me?"

Ruth remained glued to the spot as humiliation welled up within her. She realized that Steve was waiting for her reply. On his face was mirrored the same set of hopes and dreams that had filled her.

As Nicole arrived at their table, Ruth said in a low but shaky voice, "I'll see what I can do."

Nicole kissed and hugged them both. When she pulled away from Steve, Ruth did not miss the look of adoration on his face. It was most likely the same look she'd had on her own. How could she have been so stupid?

"Can I get you a drink?" Steve asked Nicole.

"That'd be great. Draft beer is fine."

And off Steve went to do Nicole's bidding, Ruth observed, just like every other man who had come into her sister's orbit.

"I thought you weren't coming out tonight?"

Ruth asked, hoping her sister didn't notice the edge in her voice.

Nicole shrugged, looking around the place to see who was there. Without looking at Ruth, she answered, "I changed my mind."

Ruth gathered her purse and looped it over her shoulder. Steve was working his way back toward them carrying two pint glasses of beer.

"You're not going, are you?" Nicole asked, almost indignant. "I just got here."

Biting her tongue, Ruth refrained from telling her that *she* was the reason she was leaving. Her leg began to throb. She needed go home. "My leg is aching."

Nicole nodded in understanding.

Ruth cast a forlorn glance back at Steve and turned back toward her sister. "Nicole, I think Steve has a crush on you."

Nicole smiled. "Really? He's kind of cute. Is he nice?"

Ruth nodded.

"Why doesn't he ask me out?" she asked.

"I think he's shy," Ruth said. Suddenly, she felt weary.

Nicole beamed. "Then I'll help him along."

Ruth said a quick good night and slipped out the door.

~

THE DECISION TO park a couple of blocks away didn't seem so wise now. It felt as if all Ruth's emotions had leaked out of her heart and pooled into her right leg. She limped toward her car, biting her lip to try and quell the tears that threatened to break the dam of disappointment.

Lights flashed from Java Joe's, the local coffee spot. On impulse, she pulled open the door and breathed in deeply the smell of fresh-brewed coffee. A few old men lined the counter. In unison, they looked toward her and then went back to their coffee cups. At the counter, she ordered a large tea and a biscotti, then wound her way to the back of the restaurant and chose a table by the window. She draped her sweater over the back of her chair and sat down, and it wasn't long before the waitress set her order down in front of her. Ruth stared listlessly out the window.

The irony of her situation was not lost on her. Here she was, a romance writer of all things, and she couldn't even manage to land a date, much less a man. She wrote about falling in love and happily-ever-after, but in her personal life, those things were elusive. How on earth was she supposed to write about romance when she had none of her own? It made her feel like a fraud.

She wasn't beastly; she was fairly attractive, she knew, but she supposed there might be some men who were put off by her limp. She had had boyfriends in the past, but it had never amounted to anything serious.

Her father had told her, more than once, "There is someone out there for you, Ruth. There are over seven billion people on the planet. For every Jack there's a Jill." But she was seriously beginning to doubt that.

Sometimes, Ruth despaired of ever meeting anyone.

She picked up her tea and sipped it, breathing in the welcoming fragrance. As she did, she spied Nicole and Steve making their way down the sidewalk, arm in arm. Nicole threw her head back and laughed at something Steve said. Ruth panicked; she didn't want either of them to see her sitting there alone. How pathetic was that? She grabbed a discarded newspaper from the seat next to her and opened it up, hiding behind the pages as they walked past. After a few moments, when she was sure they were gone, she began to lower the paper, but something caught her eye and she frowned.

At the bottom of page eight, in the right-hand

corner, was a plain black-and-white box ad that read:

*The Clonmel Marriage Bureau*
*Making Introductions since 1978*
*Discretion Assured*
*"Falling in Love the Old-Fashioned Way"*
*Mrs. Margaret Murphy*
*Cashel Road*
*Clonmel*
*County Tipperary*
*Ireland*

RUTH SAT UP STRAIGHTER. She closed the paper, reading the title. It was a newspaper for Irish expats living in the US. She pulled her phone from her purse and quickly googled the Clonmel Marriage Bureau.

They did not have a website, but Mrs. Murphy had done a few print interviews. Ruth clicked on the first article and scanned it, devouring the information. It was a matchmaking service with a traditional matchmaker. Mrs. Murphy had been running the bureau for nearly four decades, and had over one thousand marriages to her credit.

Ruth sat back in her chair and read on, her tea, biscotti, and the pain in her leg forgotten. Mrs. Murphy advised any interested parties to write a letter to her in care of the Bureau and enclose a picture. She believed in love, and that's all she needed. Using her phone, Ruth snapped a picture of the ad, then tucked it safely in her purse before pulling her sweater off the back of the chair and heading home.

The night hadn't been a total loss. She'd just found an idea for her next book.

# CHAPTER TWO

Sean Hughes stood behind the bar of the pub he'd inherited from his parents. His pub, called Off the Beaten Track, was located right in the middle of Ireland, in an area referred to as the Golden Vale.

Toothpick dangling from the corner of his mouth, he thumbed through a catalogue, looking at apple and pear trees for his orchard. At the same time, he kept a watchful eye on the old man at the end of the bar. Mackie had been married to Sean's aunt, and since her death five years ago, the old fella had been a little lost. Sean felt compelled to look after him.

"How ye doin' down at your end of the bar, Mackie?" Sean called out to him.

Charles "Mackie" McDonald nodded and lifted his pint glass. "One more for the road, lad," he replied.

Sean filled Mackie's glass and set it in front of him. Although only related by marriage, he was fond of his uncle. Mackie had been married to Carmel, the sister of Sean's mother. The pity was, they had had no children of their own, but they had doted on Sean and his older brothers, Connor and Tommy. Sean had spent many a happy day at Mackie and Carmel's farm.

Seated along the bar were the usual customers: Moss, the village postman; the undertaker, Calvin; and two farmers, Seamus and John Joe. In a corner sat a gaggle of girls who flirted with Sean when they ordered their drinks. He paid no mind to them. People did all sorts of stupid things when they had the drink in them. As for himself, he didn't touch the stuff. He'd seen enough of what it did to people. His mother used to say there was demon in the drink for some. And he agreed.

His staff of one, Marie, a widow in her fifties, stood on the other side of the bar, showing the patrons a grainy black-and-white sonogram image of her soon-to-be first grandchild. Marie was beaming from ear to ear.

Moss turned the photo around and squinted.

"It's hard to make it out, Marie. We might wait and have a look when the baby gets here." Shrugging, he passed it to Calvin. The undertaker studied it over his pint glass.

"Look at his little hands," Marie enthused, not to be dissuaded by Moss's lack of interest.

Sean watched from the corner of his eye as Calvin glanced shyly at Marie and then rotated the photo, looking for the appendages in question. Calvin, a widower, had a bit of a crush on Marie. But Sean thought either Marie was oblivious, or it was too soon after her husband's death. "Where?" Calvin asked.

Marie looked at the picture and immediately frowned. "Why you blooming eejit! You've got it upside down." Impatient, she righted it.

Calvin responded with an "oh," and cast a sidelong glance at Marie. He studied it again and said with a chuckle, "I thought that was his bum; it looked a little big. But it's his head."

"Does this picture make my bum look big?" Seamus asked, and all the men lined up at the bar laughed. And despite the look on Marie's face, another chuckle escaped from Calvin.

Grabbing the picture from his hand, she studied it again herself and smiled proudly before carefully folding it up and placing it in her apron pocket.

She turned sharply toward them. "You're nothing but a bunch of blaguards. Now, hurry up and finish so I can tidy up and go home!" She snapped a dishtowel on the bar and they all sat up a little straighter.

Sean grinned. Marie was barely five foot, but she managed to keep everyone in line. As she disappeared into the kitchen, Calvin whispered in admiration, "She's mighty fierce for someone so small."

Sean shook his head and began to clear the tables.

The girls in the corner laughed a little too loudly, and Sean glanced at the clock. Only twenty minutes until closing time.

His dog, an Irish border collie named Shep who had been sound asleep at the foot of Mackie's bar stool, lifted his head at the sound of the girls' laughter. He observed them for a moment, decided they didn't bear watching, and laid his head back down with a groan and closed his eyes.

"Tommy and Dorothy might be coming down for the weekend with the baby," Sean said, referring to his older brother, his wife, and their baby daughter.

As if reading his mind, Mackie said, "Maybe

Dorothy will bring down some of that Victoria sponge she makes."

Sean leaned on the bar. "We can only hope."

"My Carmel used to make a beautiful sponge," Mackie said quietly. "I miss her."

"Ah, we all miss Carmel," Sean answered truthfully. "She was someone worth missing."

"You need to find someone for yourself," Mackie said, tilting the pint glass up to his lips.

Sean smiled at him. "All the good ones are taken."

This was a regular conversation between them: his octogenarian uncle trying to encourage him to get a girlfriend, or worse, get married. *Been there, done that*, Sean thought.

"But you might have a better chance if you get rid of the beard and mustache," Mackie said. This was also an ongoing topic. Mackie was old-school, which also meant clean-shaven. Sean fingered his beard and appeared to be deep in thought.

"I'll take it under consideration."

Mackie waved his hand away. "Ah go on, lad, you tell me that every time I bring it up."

Sean laughed.

"Beard or no beard, mark my words, your time will come. You'll be hit by a thunderbolt. And you'll just know. Just like it was for me when I first laid my eyes on Carmel." Mackie paused for a moment and stared at his brew as if it held all the answers. "Did I ever tell you about the night I first met Carmel? At the dance at the crossroads?"

Sean smiled, leaned across the bar, and said to his uncle, "You may have mentioned it once or twice. Tell me again."

Mackie launched into the story from years ago, when things were a lot simpler and he had laid eyes on a dark-haired girl at a dance.

When his uncle was finished reminiscing, Sean glanced up at the clock above the cash register and called out in a deep voice. "Pub's closed."

His patrons finished their drinks and began to head out. The girls in the corner stood up but seemed to be lingering. Sean stepped over to the brass bell bolted to the post and rang it, indicating it was time to go. When the girls still showed no sign of leaving, he whistled for the dog. Shep stood up and looked at him expectantly. "Move them out," he ordered the dog, nodding his head toward the girls in the corner.

The dog trotted over to the trio of girls and began to circle around their feet. Behind them, he began to press at their heels, and automatically, they moved forward.

"What is he doing?" one of them asked in a

shrill voice, as the dog kept them moving toward the door.

"Herding," Sean said with a grin and a shrug. "He can't help it. It's in his genes."

The girls got the message and stumbled out of the pub with Shep on their heels.

"Careful now," Sean called out after them.

Once the pub was empty, Sean wiped down the bar with a damp rag and waited for his uncle to get his coat and cap on.

"C'mon, Mackie, I'll give you a lift home," he said.

"I can walk," Mackie said.

"I know you can, but I'm in the mood for a drive," Sean said. He'd been giving his uncle a lift home for the past three years. This had become their routine.

His uncle drained the rest of his glass and slid it across the bar. Sean caught it and set it in the sink.

He called for the dog to wait outside until he returned. If it should rain, there was a doghouse out back he could take shelter in. As they walked out, Sean flipped the lights off and locked the door behind him. He slid into the driver's seat of his Toyota, and his uncle climbed in the passenger side.

Mackie began to sing some long-forgotten song from his childhood. Sean grinned as he shifted the car into gear and pulled out of the paved parking lot.

It was a starry night, and the sky above twinkled. That was one of the things Sean loved about living in the rural area: the clear, bright night skies and the peace and solitude. He drove the car expertly around the bends and up and down the dips, but there was no worry; the country roads were quiet this time of night.

Mackie paused his singing. "Pull over lad, so I can hit this high note."

Sean obliged his uncle and pulled the car over to the edge of the road. He had to be careful as there was a three-foot drainage ditch next to the asphalt.

Once the verses were sung and the high notes reached, Sean threw the car back into gear and pulled out onto the narrow country lane.

After five minutes, he turned left down a long, narrow passageway known as a boreen. There were neighboring cottages along the way, but Mackie lived in a farmhouse at the end. As they pulled in, the beams from Sean's headlights swept across the stone cottage, and his uncle's Jack Russell terrier came tearing around the corner, barking his head off.

Sean stepped out of the car, pulled a dog biscuit

from the inside well of the car door and threw it to him. "Easy, Sparky, it's just the boss who's come home." Sean made his way around the car to where his uncle had stepped out, and followed him into the cottage, making sure he got in all right.

Mackie turned on the hall light, and Sean followed him into the kitchen. He grabbed the kettle off the range and filled it up. His uncle liked a strong cup of tea before going to bed.

"Will ye have a cup of tea before you go?" Mackie asked, pulling down a small teapot.

"Ah, sure, one for the road," Sean answered. He pulled a jug of milk from the fridge as his uncle spooned loose tea into a tea ball and placed it in the teapot.

Once the kettle boiled, Sean lifted it from the range and poured water into the teapot.

He sat down with his uncle at the kitchen table with the oilcloth tablecloth, fixed their tea to their liking, and sat back and had a sip. They spoke of the coalition government and Tipperary's chances next year in the all-Ireland. Sometimes, Sean thought, there were no more pleasurable ways to pass the time than with a strong cup of tea, good conversation, and good company.

# CHAPTER THREE

"What is all this mail coming from Ireland?" Bill Davenport asked his daughter, peering over the top of his glasses. His features were grizzled and his hair short and gray, but whenever he looked at his oldest daughter his countenance automatically softened.

Her father stood at the sink in the kitchen. There was a smell of fresh-brewed coffee, which Ruth always found comforting. She smiled and pulled three envelopes from her dad's hand. "It's just research for my next book, Dad."

Since that night she'd spotted the ad for the marriage bureau, her imagination had gone into overdrive and with it, her idea for her newest book. Based loosely on personal experience, her next novel was going to be about a girl who had difficulty finding love in the US, stumbled upon an international matchmaking service, and found the man of her dreams in Ireland.

It had been two months since she'd first written to Mrs. Murphy of the Clonmel Marriage Bureau, explaining that she was a writer doing research on her next book. She'd inquired as to whether any of the bureau's members might agree to being interviewed via mail or email. Within weeks, Mrs. Murphy had sent a letter in response saying that she had three members who would be willing to talk to Ruth.

When Ruth had pitched the idea to her editor, Noelle had been enthused about the project. Once she established contact with the three members, Ruth began her research in earnest. She'd sent them questionnaires and was pleased when they were returned promptly. In addition, she'd begun reading everything she could about Ireland: travel blogs, tourism sites, and Irish newspapers. She'd never keep it all straight between the rugby, soccer, and hurling, but a sense of the island on the westernmost point of Europe was beginning to take shape.

With the envelopes in one hand and a mug of tea in the other, she headed toward her bedroom at the back of the house. She pulled off her daisy-print cardigan, propped up a pillow against the headboard, and leaned back against it, stretching out her legs. She looked at the three letters in her lap. One was from Declan in Killarney, one from Majella in Dublin, and one from Paul in Cork, which according to her map put them at opposite ends of the country. Ruth picked up the one from Declan, and readjusted her leg on the bed to get comfortable. She slid the letter out of the envelope, unfolded it, and smiled at the now-familiar masculine scrawl.

*Dear Ruth,*

*Your letter came yesterday and I sat in the garden to read it. After a spell of rain, we're finally enjoying the sunshine. I really enjoy your letters, Ruth. I can tell you're a sound girl . . .*

Ruth slipped into the rhythm of his letter, picturing him in his Killarney garden, surrounded by flowers. She imagined roses, geraniums, gladiolas, and dahlias. When she reached the last line of his letter, she read and reread it, her heart rate gathering speed.

. . .

*Ruth, I wondered if you'll be making the journey to Ireland to further your research? You should see Ireland firsthand, to get a true sense of the country and her people. Killarney is a great town. There's lots to do and see, and I would love to show you around.*

*Declan*

Ruth stared at his closing lines and his proposal for a long time. He had a point. To go to Ireland would certainly add authenticity to her research that she'd never get from a travel site. Biting her lip, she glanced out the window at the large maple tree in full leaf. *What harm could there be?* She could go to Ireland and do thorough research on her setting. She wondered if Majella and Paul would also agree to meet her in person. She allowed her mind to wander, considering the possibilities, until she found herself fantasizing about finding love there for herself. Giving her head a hard shake, she dislodged that thought or any like it from her mind. There wouldn't be much point in falling for a man who lived on the other side of the ocean. This was about romance, yes, but it was about writing it, not living it. Besides, after all that business with Steve, she wasn't in any hurry for a romantic entanglement.

An urgent knock at her bedroom door, followed by her sister bursting through and hopping on her bed, forced Ruth to fold up the letter and shove it back into its envelope.

"What are you doing?" Nicole asked, her blonde curls falling over her shoulders.

"Nothing," Ruth answered.

"I just wanted to thank you for fixing me up with Steve. He's a nice guy," Nicole said, blissfully unaware of the pain it had caused Ruth.

Ruth gave her a small smile. "I'm glad. He is nice." She paused. "You deserve someone nice."

"I know I do," Nicole said, then added as an afterthought, "And so do you!"

Ruth shrugged.

"Anyway, we're going out tonight and I wondered if you wanted to go with us."

Ruth stared at her younger sister. She swallowed hard. "No, that's okay. You certainly don't need me tagging along. Three on a date and all that."

Nicole rolled her eyes. "It wouldn't be like that at all. We'd all just hang out."

"Another time," Ruth said.

"Oh, come on, you haven't been out in ages," Nicole countered.

"Another time," Ruth said. "Besides, my leg is a little achy tonight."

Nicole frowned. "Is it? That hasn't happened in a while."

The last thing in the world she wanted to do was hang out with her sister and her former crush, and watch as they fell in love with each other. She'd rather walk across hot coals.

"All right then, suit yourself," Nicole said, sliding off the bed. She glanced at the letters resting beside Ruth on the bed. "Dad said you've been getting mail from Ireland?"

Ruth nodded. "Just some research for my next book."

"Oh, okay," Nicole said, and she slipped out of the room and shut the door behind her.

Ruth flipped open her laptop and googled flights to Ireland.

# CHAPTER FOUR

Sean heaved the empty beer barrel up onto his shoulder as if it were lightweight. Whistling, he carried it outdoors and laid it in front of his pub on the main street of the village. He removed the remaining barrels from the back room and added them to his collection at the curb. Pickup was before noon. He looked up toward the sun trying to break through white cloud cover, and decided it was going to be a good day. It was Monday, and it was his day off. The pub was closed.

He looked down at his Irish collie, who followed him. "What do you think, Shep? Good day for a walk?"

The dog wagged his tail in agreement and followed Sean back inside.

Danny the plumber was in the back room assessing the boiler. As he had many times before. Sean dreaded the answer, because he knew what it was likely to be, and it wouldn't be good. That boiler had been there since Sean was a kid. And although he had it serviced religiously every year, there was nothing that could be done about its age.

The plumber stood up and wiped his hands on a rag.

Sean leaned on the door frame, working the toothpick in his mouth.

"Well, what's the damage?" Sean asked. He hoped he could get away with one more winter. He was good about putting money aside, but he much preferred to invest it in his real passion: his orchard. Last year, he'd planted three hundred apple trees on land he'd leased from Mackie. He was saving for his next purchase: pear saplings. His business plan involved supplying fresh produce to grocery stores and eventually a big company like Bulmers, who'd use his fruit to make their cider. But that would require investment.

By the expression on the plumber's face, Sean already knew the answer.

"My advice would be to replace it," Danny said.

"I know, but you said that last year and the year before that," Sean pointed out.

"And I'll say it again. Look, I can service it, but what needs to be done, what I've been putting off, is going to be expensive. You might as well spring for a new one altogether."

Sean sighed. He knew it was the smart thing to do. But if he used his savings for a new boiler, then he'd have to put his dream on hold for another few years. He didn't know if he could handle that—the thought of working in the pub any longer than he had to would cause him to lose the will to live. But right now, it paid the bills.

"Bloody hell," he said, banging on the door frame.

The plumber began to pick up his tools and put them in his box. When he was finished, Sean walked him out.

"Look, just let me know what you want to do," he said at the door.

"Let me have a think about it," Sean said.

The plumber laughed. "You've been thinking about it for the last five years."

"And what was the price again?" Sean asked, knowing full well.

"Five grand," the plumber responded.

"That's what I thought." Sean grimaced.

He bolted the door behind the plumber. Despite the bad news, he was going to enjoy his day off.

Anxious to get out of the pub, he grabbed the two slim volumes of poetry tucked next to the cash register and headed out with the dog at his side.

~

"WHAT'S THE NEWS, MIRIAM?" he asked as he strolled into the local newsagents. He asked for a bacon buttie and a bag of crisps. He'd made a flask of hot tea. He was going to walk up to the top of the hill at the edge of town, park himself in his favorite spot, sip his tea, read, and enjoy the view.

Miriam had gone to London in her twenties and worked as a nurse, but had returned to Ireland after she'd retired and bought the shop from the previous owners. Now well into her seventies, she did not look as if she'd be slowing down anytime soon.

"I heard that Brid may be coming back," she said, not taking her eyes off of him. "Her father is unwell."

"Is that so?" Sean said. He knew she was looking for a comment, but he wasn't going to give her one.

Without another word, she rang up his items and told him the total. He pulled a pile of loose change from his pocket and handed her a bunch of euro coins, then picked up the sandwich and the crisps and put them in a brown paper bag.

She nodded toward the big glass window. "Enjoy the day. Looks like rain for the rest of the week."

"Is that what Met Éireann says?" Sean asked.

Miriam laughed, her eyes crinkling in the corners. "No, but it's what my knees were telling me this morning. Lot of rain coming. It's best to enjoy the day while the sun lasts."

"Will do," he said.

But Miriam wasn't ready to let him go yet. "Is it poetry that you'd be reading?"

He held up the books for her inspection. "Heaney and Hartnett."

She nodded and as he walked out, she said behind him, "We're a country of dreamers and poets."

He laughed and headed out of town. It was just after ten in the morning and the village was coming to life. White net curtains opened and dogs were let out. As he passed the local primary school, he could hear the voices of children floating out on the gentle breeze. It hadn't been that long since he himself had gone to school there, along with his older brothers. His favorite subjects had been recess and the playing of soccer in the schoolyard. That was until he'd been introduced to poetry in secondary school by his first-year English teacher, Mrs. Moriarty, and it was as if his eyes had been opened. As if he hadn't been seeing properly up until that point. These days, his mornings were dedicated to the orchard and the weekends were for rugby, soccer matches, and the local GAA. But his days off were devoted to the reading of poetry and trying to figure out how it had all been put together. And sometimes just letting the words float over him as he lay back and closed his eyes.

September was setting fast, and soon the dark evenings would be upon them. Tourism, one of the biggest industries in Ireland, was winding down, and though there would be a few stragglers, not many would venture away from the main cities and thoroughfares to explore their little village. It would be winter nights of matches, sitting by the fire, and pub nights.

Poetry books in hand and the dog trotting at his side, he ambled down the passageway toward Mackie's farmhouse. His uncle's car was gone, so Sean kept walking past the house and cut through the hedge until he stood in the field he rented from Mackie. Surrounding him were rows and rows of apple trees. Hundreds of them. With a smile on his face, he rubbed his fingers along the smooth bark of one of the trees. In a few years' time, he hoped these trees would be heavy with fruit. He walked along the rows, inspecting the trees for any damage.

Once he was satisfied, he exited the field and continued walking to the back of Mackie's property. He hopped the low stone wall at the end of his uncle's farm and made his way up the hill. He had an understanding with the neighboring farmer, Peter Fitzgerald. Sean walked though his fields to the leafy glen at the top of the hill and in return, Peter had his first drink on the house when he visited the pub, which was a few times a month. Every Monday, Peter texted him to tell him which field the bull was in. The last thing Sean needed was to run afoul of the bull.

Sean whistled an old tune as he walked along the dirt path that bordered the first field. The only sound was the munching of the grass by the cows and the swishing of their tails. Passing the second field, he caught sight of Peter in his tractor on the other side of it. The farmer put up his hand in greeting, and Sean returned the salute. After the second field, the land became a natural upward slope, and Sean felt the tug in his legs. At the crest at the top of the hill were the ruins of an old stone wall shaded by a giant oak tree. He'd previously cleared a spot against part of the wall that still stood, to protect him from the wind. He sat down and stretched out his legs, looking around below at the valley of lush green hills fenced off by low stone walls or natural hedges of whitethorn, and their village nestled in the crook of it. It was a sight he never grew tired of looking at: the Golden Vale. He smiled at the dog, who regarded him while wagging his tail.

Sean settled down in his spot under the tree with his flask of tea, his lunch, and his two slim volumes of poetry. He opened his sandwich, tore off a generous portion, and tossed it to the dog. His gaze landed on the field below with its neat rows of fruit trees. Every time he looked at it, he was content. Satisfied at the orderliness of it. But soon, dark clouds gathering on the horizon caught his attention, and he gazed westward toward the Atlantic. He couldn't help but wonder what would blow in.

# CHAPTER FIVE

Despite all her meticulous arrangements for her trip to Ireland, Ruth learned there were some things she had no control over.

The overnight flight from New York to Shannon had been smooth and uneventful until the last hour, when the plane hit turbulence. Passengers were subdued, snack service canceled, and the flight attendants strapped themselves into their seats. As the plane bounced sideways, Ruth forced herself to look out the window, not wanting to miss her first view of Ireland despite the overwhelming urge to throw up. She was rewarded with rolling, rich green fields hedged off by dark stone walls, making the west side of the country resemble a quilt. One she would prefer to crawl under right now. The slate gray skies and the pelting rain were disappointing, but she supposed that was what made it all so green.

As the final descent began, she looked heavenward and whispered a prayer. The plane rocked along on an air current and Ruth only let her breath go when the plane became level with the runway. After a bumpy landing, passengers clapped in relief as they pulled up to the gate at the Shannon airport in the west of Ireland.

"It's fourteen degrees Celsius and raining in Shannon," the pilot announced.

*No kidding.*

As much as she had anticipated this new adventure, as much as she had *needed* it, she'd begun to have doubts as soon as she'd boarded the plane. What on earth was she thinking, traveling three thousand miles by herself?

Her sister had dropped many hints about accompanying her, finally resorting to begging. Ruth had been alarmed, but held firm. The last thing she needed was to watch her sister conquer another country of men. Besides, she was there to work. Ruth had suggested somewhat slyly that Nicole wouldn't want to leave Steve in the early stages of their relationship, and Nicole had taken the bait. Her father had thought a change of scenery might do her good, and she was relieved that he didn't try to dissuade her from her journey, or worse, take Nicole's side in her effort to join Ruth. Off she traveled to Ireland. Alone.

~

RUTH FOLLOWED the rest of the passengers through the winding halls of Shannon Airport. After clearing customs, she headed toward baggage claim. Shannon was a small airport, and Ruth was grateful, as it meant not having to walk long distances. A car accident as a teenager had left her right leg badly damaged, and it was now held together by an assortment of rods, pins, and screws. But so far, it was holding up well to the journey.

She stood at the carousel, recognizing some of the people from her trans-Atlantic flight. The carousel groaned into action, the belt began to move, and it wasn't long before luggage bumped out onto the belt.

At first, Ruth didn't panic when her floral suitcase was nowhere to be seen along the conveyor belt. But after other passengers had wrestled their suitcases off of the carousel and departed one by one, Ruth was left with the sinking feeling that her luggage had been lost.

Weary and beginning to feel the effects of jet lag, she approached the first airport official she saw, who happened to be pushing a janitorial cart with all sorts of spray bottles hanging off of it into a restroom.

When Ruth explained the situation, the young blonde girl looked at her quizzically and shrugged. "No English. Sorry. Polish."

Ruth's shoulders sagged and she bit her lip. The Polish girl was pointing to an office on the other side of the concourse, and Ruth nodded and wheeled her carry-on in that direction.

Two men in white business shirts and dark pants, wearing official-looking identification tags, looked up at Ruth as she entered their office.

"I just came in on that flight from New York, and my luggage appears to be lost," Ruth said, clutching her purse close to her.

The men exchanged a look and turned back to her, regarding her with sympathy.

"Do you have the baggage claim?" asked the one sitting behind the desk.

"I do," Ruth said. She pulled out her boarding pass with the baggage claim stapled to the back of it, and handed it to him.

He put on a pair of glasses and examined her baggage receipt. Then he looked at Ruth and nodded toward the office chairs lined up against the wall. "Have a seat while we sort this out."

"Thank you," she said. She smoothed her dress and sat down.

He picked up the phone and dialed an extension. "Listen, Joe, can you check the hold for me on that flight that just came in from New York? We've got a missing piece of luggage—" He put his hand over the receiver and said to Ruth, "Can you describe it?"

"Yes, it's a dark blue floral suitcase."

The older man nodded in approval. "Well done for not having a plain black one." He removed his hand and said into the phone, "It's dark blue with flowers." He listened to the voice on the other end. "All right then, let me know." He turned back to Ruth. "They're just tidying up the plane now, and they'll have a look and get back to me." He turned to the other man, who stood with his back to the wall. "Sam, why don't you see if you can get this young lady a nice cup of tea."

The other fellow nodded and disappeared out the door before Ruth could protest. A cup of tea sounded lovely anyway. She hoped it wouldn't be too long before they located her luggage.

"You're from America," the man behind the desk said.

Ruth nodded.

"We get a lot of Americans visiting," he remarked. "Is it your first time here?"

Ruth nodded, leaning forward in her chair. Despite her fatigue, she was excited about her working vacation. She'd booked a cozy-sounding, Wi-Fi-equipped B & B right in the middle of the country, in County Tipperary. That way, she could spend the next six weeks working on her book, sightseeing around the country, and interviewing her pen pals from the marriage bureau. All three had agreed to meet up with her while she was in Ireland.

"Why are you traveling by yourself?" he asked, peering over the top of his glasses.

She sat up straighter. "I'm a writer and I'm here to do research," she replied.

"A writer? Is that so? I love to read. Mainly James Patterson and Jeffrey Archer."

"I write romance," Ruth volunteered.

She thought she saw a slight grimace but she couldn't be sure.

"The missus loves her romance," he said. "I myself don't see what all the fuss is about."

Before Ruth could respond, Sam returned with a cup of hot tea in a white china teacup. He handed it to Ruth. On the saucer were two cookies.

"There's some biscuits for you. You'll be hungry after your journey."

Ruth gratefully took the cup and sipped it. As she bit into the cookie, the phone on the desk rang. She hoped it was about her suitcase.

"McKiernan here. Yep, that's right. Okay, bye, thanks, bye, bye, bye, bye, bye," he said, hanging up the receiver.

Folding his hands on his desk, he leaned forward and looked at Ruth. "I'm sorry, but your luggage was not found."

Ruth slumped in her chair. "Now what do I do?"

"I'll contact the office in New York and give them the claim number."

It didn't warrant thinking about: her entire wardrobe and toiletries, as well as the addresses of her pen pals, were now lost somewhere between New York and Ireland.

"There is another flight coming in from New York this afternoon. You might want to wait for that one," he suggested.

It was only nine in the morning. She certainly didn't treasure the thought of hanging around the airport all day. But the B & B she had booked was hours away.

"Is there a tourist site nearby? Somewhere I can go to pass the time?"

"The Cliffs of Mohr aren't too far from here—about an hour," he answered.

"That's what I'll do," she said, lacking enthusiasm. What she wanted to do was crawl under a blanket and sleep off the jet lag. But she wanted her luggage more. "Can I leave my cell number with you? It's an American number," Ruth said.

"Er—no," he said apologetically. He pulled his business card from a case on the desk. "Here's the number for this office. You can ring this afternoon. Most likely your case is still in New York and if that is true, it'll be over on the next flight."

She finished her tea. "Where are the rental car offices?"

"Sam will show you. As soon as you exit the baggage claim area, you'll see them."

She stood up and placed the empty cup and saucer on his desk, thanking both of them for their assistance.

On the way out, she glanced at the arrivals board to see the time of the next flight from New York. It wasn't due until three. That was still six hours away. Once she'd secured a rental car with her credit card, she bought a large cup of black coffee and headed out the door, pulling her carry-on behind her. Heading toward the bay of rental cars, she began to feel excited and invigorated despite the mishap with the missing luggage.

Carefully, she placed her small suitcase in the backseat. Thank God she had packed a change of clothes and a pair of clean underwear. She could pick up some toiletries in one of the local shops.

She slid into the driver's seat, which was on the right side, and familiarized herself with the car. She scrolled through her phone for Google Maps, then typed in "The Cliffs of Mohr." She slowly reversed her car out of the parking spot.

It took Ruth awhile to get used to driving on the opposite side of the road. Each time she approached a roundabout—and there were plenty—she stopped and said to herself, "Stop, look right, and go, if clear."

She drove cautiously and let people pass her. It was raining and she wasn't familiar with the roads. Despite the rain and the overcast sky, she fell in love with the scenery. Hilly, lush, grassy, and green, it was mesmerizing, but she forced herself to pay attention to the road.

~

THE CLIFFS of Mohr were sea cliffs located on the western side of the country, overlooking the Atlantic.

At their tallest point, they were over seven hundred feet in height. A gray mist enveloped the place, giving it an otherworldly appearance. Ruth stood there and sucked in a deep breath, feeling giddy. She hugged herself not only in an effort to keep warm, but from a feeling of being happy. A shiver went down her spine, caused by an innate feeling that this was going to be a good trip. She pulled her cell phone from the pocket of her cardigan and began to snap pictures. She watched other tourists in their raincoats and thought about her own, packed securely in her lost suitcase. Her cardigan began to get damp, and reluctantly she moved inside to the visitor center to get warm.

Doolin was a little tourist town not too far from the cliffs. Before long, she found herself in a dark, quiet little pub where she had a bowl of cream of potato and leek soup and some warmed brown bread. Hungry, she ate everything that was laid down in front of her and finished it off with two cups of hot tea. After a while, she began to yawn, and forced herself to stand up and head back to the car.

Ruth settled into the driver's seat and stared straight ahead. Before she'd even started the ignition, jet lag overpowered her and she nodded off.

~

When she awoke, it was after three. She hurriedly drove to the airport to find that the plane from New York had been delayed. Ruth collapsed onto a hard plastic chair just outside of the arrivals gate and passed the hour fighting to stay awake. When the plane arrived, she rang the number on the business card. The man told her he'd check for her luggage and let her know.

She sat back down and waited, watching passengers disembark and exit through the doors from baggage claim. She scanned all the luggage wheeled by her, making sure her suitcase wasn't among them. The last thing she needed was to add "stolen" to her list. Soon she saw the friendly face of the airport worker who had helped her earlier, and she smiled and waved to draw his attention. Her heart sank when she saw that he was empty-handed.

He wore an apologetic smile. "I'm sorry, your suitcase didn't come in on that flight."

She groaned.

"I'll continue to look for it, and you can ring me every morning for an update," he said. "You have my card."

She nodded, dejected. It was getting late and she still had the drive to the B & B ahead of her. She'd like to arrive there before it got dark. Ruth thanked him again and headed back out to the parking lot. There was nothing more that could be done that day. She'd figure it out in the morning after a good night's sleep.

# CHAPTER SIX

It was dark by the time Ruth arrived in County Tipperary. She drove past the B & B three times without seeing it, the illuminated white sign with the black lettering obscured by a big, old sycamore tree.

Finally, bone tired, she pulled her car into the asphalt space in front of the two-story house. There were several other cars parked out front. There was a glass vestibule off the entrance, and she slid it open and stepped inside. She knocked on the door and waited.

A middle-aged woman appeared at the door with a welcoming smile. "Can I help you?" she asked. Her hair was dark, and she wore minimal makeup. There was the smell of home cooking in the air, and Ruth's stomach growled in response.

"Hi, I'm Ruth Davenport. I have a reservation."

The woman frowned. "I'm sorry, but we're full. What did you say your name was again?" She opened the door wider and indicated to Ruth to follow her into the front hall.

Ruth's shoulders sagged. "Ruth Davenport. I made arrangements to stay the week."

The woman looked at her quizzically. "Oh right, you're from America. But I have you in my books as coming next Monday."

"No, it's this Monday," Ruth said. She looked around the hallway. It was done up in carpet with a diamond pattern, and there was striped, patterned wallpaper covering the walls, which were adorned with framed prints of Irish landscapes. A dark, ornate banister on the staircase led to the upstairs. The overall feel was cozy, just as Ruth had expected.

"Let me check," the woman said.

She went to a small counter behind the desk and put on her glasses. She clicked her computer mouse a couple of times and turned the screen so Ruth could view it.

"Here's the contact form you filled out online," she said.

Ruth's heart sank. There in black and white was

the form she had submitted. But with next week's date.

Ruth groaned. How had that happened? And why hadn't she confirmed it?

"I suppose you don't have anything for me to rent?"

The woman shook her head. "I am sorry. We're full up this week. But I do have you down for next week."

Ruth pointed out the obvious. "Yes, but I need somewhere to stay for tonight."

The woman looked at her thoughtfully. "Right then. Here's what you do. Drive out of here, make a right and stay on the main road. You'll go through two villages and after the second village, as soon as you come out of it, you'll take a left at the fork in the road. The first house on the right is the Emerald Isle B & B. I just spoke to Maggie this morning and she had vacancies. Let me call her to make sure."

Ruth waited while the phone call was made, and once she was assured that there was indeed a room for her two villages away, she set back out on the road.

Dragging her carry-on behind her, she stepped back outside. She turned to the B & B owner and asked, "How long will it take to get there by car?"

The woman appeared thoughtful for a moment.

"About half an hour." She paused and then added, "Approximately."

Ruth stowed her carry-on behind the driver's seat and climbed back into the car. With a final wave to the proprietor of the B & B, she pulled back out onto the main road and headed in the direction she had been told.

IT WAS GROWING DARKER, and exhaustion soon washed over Ruth. Doubts began to assail her as to the wisdom of her journey. Here she was in the middle of nowhere, trying to find a place to lay her weary head. She had had better ideas. It had been a long and disappointing first day in Ireland. More determined than ever to have a successful journey, she reminded herself that she was intelligent and able-bodied, and it wouldn't be long before she'd be in a comfortable bed.

The wind picked up, as did the rain, an insistent drumbeat against the windshield. Ruth hunched over and gripped the steering wheel, peering out into the darkness. There were no streetlights, and she soon found herself on a narrow country road, bordered on both sides with drainage ditches and hedged rows of blackthorn. She slowed down in response to the weather. When she came to a fork in the road, she momentarily panicked. The woman had said the fork in the road was after the second village, and she hadn't even arrived at the first village yet. She tried to see if there were markings in the road, but there was nothing. There were no signposts, either. It was maddening. She glanced in her rearview mirror to make sure there was no one behind her. She had no idea where she was. Her stomach tightened. The car idled as Ruth bit her lip, trying to make a decision. Finally, she veered off to the right and hoped for the best.

She drove slowly. The only sound was the scraping of the wiper blades against the windshield. In the distance, she saw a cluster of lights. Relief flooded her. She relaxed her grip on the steering wheel a bit, just about wanting to cry with joy. This surely must be the village the woman had talked about. And just in time, too, as the rain and wind had picked up considerably, and she found the driving was getting to her. Then suddenly she went around a bend, and the far-off lights disappeared. One moment they were there, and then they weren't. Blackness covered the countryside like a blanket. Ruth blinked hard.

Coming around another winding bend, the tiny village reappeared and Ruth smiled to herself. She was almost there. But she hit a slick spot on the road and felt the control of the car slipping away from her. In an attempt to regain control, she tightened her grip on the steering wheel. This proved futile and the car, on a slight decline, picked up speed and slid perilously close to the edge of the road, and more specifically, to the two-foot drainage ditch that ran parallel to it. Her eyes widened as the car hit some loose gravel, hydroplaned over the ditch, and crashed through an electric wire fence, which slowed the car down considerably until it rolled to a stop with a loud bang against a tree.

Stunned, she sat there for a moment, frozen to the seat, her mouth hanging open. Through the windshield, she could see the hood of the car was crumpled. She groaned. She hadn't even been in Ireland twelve hours and she'd already lost her suitcase and totaled the rental car.

*Don't cry*. She had to focus and figure a way out of this mess. She paid attention to her body. There were no obvious cuts or bruises, and nothing hurt. That was the good news. But the accident had shaken her up.

There wasn't much she could do. Surely, a car would pass and help her out.

Ruth sat there in the car for twenty minutes, and

not a single vehicle went by. She shivered in her cardigan and dress. Sighing, she resigned herself to the fact that she was going to have to walk to the village. She told herself it wasn't that far. The thought of walking down a country road in a dress and lugging a carry-on behind her did not thrill her, but she had been left with no choice. She tried to open her door, but the frame had been too severely dented. Groaning, she shifted the carry-on from behind her seat to the passenger side of the car. Climbing over the console between the two front seats, she winced as she maneuvered her tall frame in the tight confines. Once in the passenger side of the front seat, she tried the door, relieved when it opened without difficulty. She pulled her carry-on out from the backseat.

She stepped out into prickly grass that scratched at her ankles and the tops of her feet. Looking down at her flats, she realized she wasn't wearing ideal footwear for walking. But then she hadn't guessed she'd be in her current predicament.

A ditch stood between her and the road. Ruth stared at it, trying to figure out how to navigate it. At the bottom of it, she could see about three inches of murky water. *That's just what I need: to land in dirty water with scratches and cuts on my feet and pick up a microbe.*

She gave a little whine when she realized that she'd have to leap over it to get to the road. She picked up her carry-on and tossed it over the ditch with a great heave and a grunt. It landed hard on the road, but that was okay; at least it was on the other side of the ditch.

Hands on her hips, she looked down at her bad leg. "It's one jump. We can do this." Her clothes were getting wetter by the minute, and she shivered.

She took a deep breath, leapt into the air, and came down on the other side, the impact causing her to catch her breath between her teeth and let out a weak "Oomph." Her bad leg had slowed her progress and she didn't quite make the road, but she landed on the other side of the ditch, her legs sliding down until both her feet were in the cold, muddy water.

*Do not cry! You can have a good cry later when you're tucked up in a nice, comfy bed.*

"Meow!" The sound of a cat in the dark field behind her startled Ruth, and she grabbed at anything she could find and scrabbled up the side of the muddy bank.

Finally on the road, she stood for a minute to catch her breath, bent over at the waist. Glancing down, she saw that her bare legs were covered in mud and scratches. Without actually seeing it, she knew her hair was a lost cause. Her dress was torn on the side, revealing a bit of leg. She swore. The dress, white with big purple flowers on it, had been her favorite.

She looked back at the rental car smashed against the tree and groaned. There was nothing she could do about that now. She'd deal with it in the morning.

When she righted her carry-on, she noticed that one of the wheels was bent. She tried rolling it along, but the broken wheel impeded its progress. Giving it a kick, she grabbed the handle and headed toward the lights of the village, half dragging, half carrying her small piece of luggage.

WHAT RUTH HAD THOUGHT WAS a village was really no more than a small gathering of buildings. There was a post office, with the distinct green-and-gold sign reading *An Post*. That was darkened. There was a small shop next to it, with the only light coming from a refrigerated cooler inside. The stone church with the tall spire, across from the shops, was shrouded in darkness, as was the rectory next door.

It was a village, all right, but everything appeared to be closed up for the night. Disheartened, she looked toward the village's only pub, which was at the bottom of the road.

Dragging her suitcase, she walked over to it, her dress and cardigan now soaked. The pub was darkened, but there were lights on upstairs. A newer-model Toyota Corolla was parked outside. A weathered sign hung next to the door reading *Off the Beaten Track Pub and B & B*. Looking around the place, Ruth didn't know if the owner was being literal or ironic. Ruth wanted to weep for the sight of it. In fresh paint below it read, *Sean Hughes, Proprietor.* There were no other cars around, and she was hopeful there would be a room for her here. She glanced up at the second floor with its window boxes of geraniums, still profuse and vibrant despite it being late September. Lights flooded the pub's marquee across the top.

She looked up at it, thinking it wasn't the most inviting place she'd ever seen, but it did have the seal of the Irish Tourist Board next to it. She tried the door, but it was locked. Closing her eyes, she tried knocking. There was no answer. She kept knocking, and eventually, she heard a dog barking from within the depths of the place.

The rain began to lash down, soaking Ruth. She leaned against the door with her fingers splayed.

She stepped back and looked up again at the lights on upstairs. As this place seemed to be her last hope, she made a fist and banged on the door.

From inside, a distinctly male voice called, “We’re closed.”

Ruth stepped back. “I can see that, but I need some help.”

There was silence for a moment and finally, to her great relief, she heard the deadbolts sliding open.

The pub door opened and a tall, dark-haired man filled the doorway. Not much older than herself, he wore a neatly trimmed beard and mustache. The toothpick he had been chewing fell from his mouth at the sight of her. There was a hint of mischief in his eyes as he regarded her with a grin and asked, “What the hell happened to you?”

# CHAPTER SEVEN

Sean Hughes stared at the flame-haired American on his doorstep. He guessed her hair was red; it was hard to tell with it being drenched. Black streaks of mascara trailed from her eyes down her cheeks. She wore an outrageous frock that certainly wasn't suited for rainy Irish weather. The dress was torn, and mud covered both it and her legs.

She needed assistance, all right. He took in the sight of her and repressed a grin. She didn't look like she was in the mood for humor, but he was sure there was a good story behind her current plight.

He opened the door and allowed her to step inside, noting that she was shivering.

"What are you doing walking out in this kind of

weather?" he asked, trying not to notice the way the wet dress clung to the curves of her tall frame.

He did not miss the irritation in her voice when she answered, "It's not by choice, I assure you. I've had an accident up the road."

"Are you hurt?" he asked. He gave her a quick once-over. She didn't appear injured, just beat up.

"No, I don't think so."

"Where's your car now? Is it blocking the road?"

She shook her head. "No, it's in a field. Sort of."

"Sort of?" he repeated. It was either in a field or it wasn't. But she probably didn't want to argue the finer points. She looked as if she couldn't handle much more. "All right, it's fine until morning. Nothing to be done about it now in the dark."

"I'm looking for a room."

He was shaking his head before she even had the whole sentence out of her mouth. His mother and father had operated the B & B when they were alive, but after their deaths, Sean had decided to get out of the accommodations business.

"I'm sorry, the B & B is no longer operational. It's only the pub now."

"But your sign . . ."

"Yeah, I really need to get a new one."

"You should take it down," she said indignantly.

"I haven't gotten around to it yet," he said. Typical tourist, he thought. Thought they could just walk in and take over. "Besides, everyone in town knows that we no longer offer accommodation."

"But I'm not from town!" she said.

"Have you tried the Blackthorn Lodge?" he asked. "It's just up the road."

"I just came from there. She's booked. She gave me the name of another place, but I can't seem to find it."

"What's the name of it?"

"The Emerald Isle B & B."

He nodded. He knew it. "It's a bit of a journey from here. You must have taken a wrong turn."

"Do you think?" she asked wearily. She was shivering violently, and he thought if she didn't get out of those wet clothes she'd end up with pneumonia.

"Are you sure you don't have anywhere I could stay, just for tonight? I'd be more than willing to pay you a fair price," she said. "I'd even pay double the fair price." Her pretty green eyes were pleading.

"Nah, look, I'll ring you a cab and they can take you over to the nearest B & B," he offered.

She hung her head and her wet red hair covered

her face like a curtain. Soon she was hiccoughing as great big sobs wracked her body.

Sean became alarmed. “Oh, for the love of all that is holy, don’t start crying!” Panic filled him.

She lifted her head and launched into a rant, flailing her arms like a windmill. It was hard to understand what she was saying through the blubbering. Something about lost luggage, a wrecked car, no place to stay, far away from home, tired and all alone. He got the gist of it.

Against his better judgement, he said with a sigh, “All right, I’ll let you a room for the night.”

She sniffled. “You will? Oh, thank you. I’ll pay cash upfront if you like,” she said.

“That’s fine,” he said.

They agreed on a price, and for the first time since he opened the door, she smiled. She had beautiful teeth. The Americans always did. Self-consciously, he ran his tongue over his own. They weren’t perfectly straight, but they were all there, and that had to count for something. He went to lift her battered carry-on, but he noticed she was still shivering. As she remained standing in the middle of his pub, dripping water and mud all over his floor, he stepped behind the counter silently and poured her a small glass of Irish whiskey. He brought it over and handed it to her.

She downed it in one gulp and wiped her mouth with the back of her hand. "Thank you."

"You're welcome," he said. "Is that all your luggage?"

She nodded. "Until the airline finds my suitcase."

"First time in Ireland?" he asked, climbing the staircase with the American following behind him.

"Yes, it is," she replied.

"Not off to a good start then, are ye?" he asked.

"No, I'm afraid not," she said.

Shep stood waiting for them at the top of the stairs, wagging his tail.

Sean reached down and rubbed the dog's ear. "Easy does it, boy."

He sensed the American's hesitation. "Does he bite?" she asked, not taking her eyes off of the dog. Shep approached her, sniffing.

"If he did, he'd have done it already," Sean replied.

"Can I pet him?"

"If you want to," he said, shrugging.

She reached out and gingerly placed her fingertips on Shep's head, then quickly removed her hand.

"Have you never had a dog?"

She shook her head. "No, my sister has allergies."

He left it at that and led her down the hall toward the guest rooms, which he kept ready for his brothers' frequent visits with their families.

He didn't know why, but he gave her the nicest room they had. After her day, he figured she could do with a bit of cheering up. His mother used to call it the Queen's room. It was all done up in pink floral wallpaper and it was the only guest room where the woodwork had been painted white. There was a double bed covered with a wool blanket and a pink quilt. The window had a view of the farm that bordered the pub out back.

He watched her intently as she surveyed the room. When her eyes landed on the bed, another tear slipped down her cheek.

Sean stiffened. "I know it's not the Ritz, but it's warm and clean," he said. What did these Americans expect?

She was shaking her head. She looked up at him. "I'm sorry. It's been a long day and to be so close to climbing into a bed . . . I'm just so grateful." She paused and her eyes swept around the room. "It's perfect."

Sean swallowed. "All right then."

"I'm sorry, again. I tend to be emotional," she said.

"I did not notice that," he said with a wink.

She held out her hand. "I'm Ruth Davenport."

He reached out and shook her hand. "Nice to meet you, Ruth Davenport. I'm Sean Hughes, owner of this establishment. You'll probably want to tidy up. The water is turned off in the shower here, but the toilet works. There's a bathroom at the other end of the hall."

She smiled. "Could you show me where it is?"

"Follow me," he said.

She gathered her toothbrush and the one set of clean clothes from her carry-on.

He led the way down to the other end of the hall and held open the bathroom door, revealing a claw-foot tub, toilet, and sink. There was a shower stall in the corner.

She looked up at him shyly. "Um, I have no toiletries."

He looked at her, not comprehending.

"You know," she started, her eyes meeting his. He wasn't sure he'd seen eyes in that deep shade of green before. "Shampoo, soap."

"Right. It's in your lost luggage?" he asked.

When she nodded, he said, "Just help yourself.

There's clean towels and facecloths in the hot press."

"Hot press?" she repeated.

He laughed. Even though they spoke the same language, things were getting lost in translation. He turned and opened the hall closet, gesturing toward the linens and towels on slatted shelves, tucked beside an insulated copper hot-water tank. He pulled down a clean towel and facecloth and handed them to her.

"They're so warm and lovely," she said, smiling.

"That's why they call it a hot press," he explained.

She went into the bathroom and closed the door behind her. Sean stood there for a few moments in the hall, staring at the door and wondering what the hell had just blown into his pub. When he heard the water for the tub running, he headed back to the kitchen, whistling. This was going to be interesting.

SEAN LOOKED up from his newspaper when Ruth appeared in the doorway. With her hair toweled in a turban, her clear, alabaster skin, and the arched eyebrows over those green eyes, his first thought was that she looked like a modern-day Boudica. He'd forgotten what it was like to have a woman around. It had been a long time. He stood abruptly from his chair, setting the paper down.

She held up her soiled clothes. "I was wondering if I might use your washer?"

He led her to a small room off the kitchen and opened the door of the front-loading wash machine. She put her clothes inside.

"It will need to go on a gentle cycle," she said.

He laughed. "I'm afraid there's only one cycle on this old girl: wash." He did not miss the confusion on her face. "Don't worry; it'll be fine."

"You don't have a dryer," she remarked, looking around.

"Don't need one. I either hang the wet clothes outside or in front of the range."

She nodded but didn't say anything. As he followed her out to the kitchen, he noticed she was limping.

"Are you hurt?" he asked.

She shook her head. "It's an old injury."

"Do you need anything for it?" he asked. She was kind of young to be limping like that, he thought. He wondered what the injury was.

"No, thank you, a good night's sleep is all I need," she said.

"Sit down for a minute, Ruth Davenport, I've fixed you something to eat," he said.

"You didn't have to go to all that trouble," she said.

"It was no trouble at all," he answered. "Have a seat."

He watched her as she tentatively took in the kitchen: the big Aga range that his parents had put in years ago, the oak table and chairs, the Belfast sink and the Formica countertops. The countertops were littered with clean crockery, seed catalogues, and books about apple trees and growing. There was parsley, mint, and thyme growing in various pots on the windowsills. In the corner was his mother's Christmas cactus, which would soon need its own room. He wondered how it would all look to an American. Then he decided he didn't care. He ladled some carrot-and-parsnip soup into a big bowl and laid it in front of her. She looked pale, and he wondered if that was her normal color or if she was ill. There was a small tray of brown bread that he slid across the table to her.

"Thank you," she said quietly. She bent her head and eagerly shoveled a spoonful of soup into her mouth. She took two pieces of bread and slathered butter over them.

When she finished the soup, he asked, "Would you like more?"

She hesitated, looking to the pot on the stove, then to him. She seemed to be wrestling with something internally. Without waiting for an answer, he took her bowl and filled it again. When she finished that off, he raised his eyebrows. The woman certainly had a great appetite.

"Thank you so much," she said. "That was delicious."

"Time for tea," he said, pouring boiling water over a few tea bags in a pot.

He took some teacups down from the old French dresser in the corner. He took milk out of the fridge and laid it on the table next to the sugar.

"How about a sweet?" he asked. "I've got a bit of apple tart, or there's some Victoria sponge that my sister-in-law made."

She perked up. "What is a Victoria sponge?" It was the first time she'd been animated since he'd opened the door for her, and he had to suppress a laugh. This American had a great appetite and a fondness for sweets, too, apparently.

"It's cake with a jam-and-cream filling."

"Oh, I'll try that," she said. Turning his back to her, he couldn't help but smile as he pulled the cake plate out of the fridge. As he did, the dog slinked over to Ruth. Sean caught him out of the corner of his eye. “Shep, no.”

Ruth reached out her hand and patted the dog. “He’s all right.”

Sean cut two slices, plated them up, and joined her at the table.

She took a forkful, closed her eyes, and announced, “It’s yummy. Very light.”

“Yes, it is ‘yummy,’” he said, amused. He sipped his tea. “What brings you all this way to Ireland by yourself? And in the off-season?”

“I’m a writer, and I’m here to do a bit of research for my next book.” She finished the last bite of sponge, pushed her plate away, and lifted her teacup to her lips for a sip.

“And what is it that you write?” he asked.

“I write romance novels.”

He grinned. “Romance is it? Hearts and flowers and stuff?”

Her smile disappeared. “Yes, hearts and flowers and all that stuff.”

“And do you make a living doing this?” he enquired. He folded his arms across his chest.

“Yes, as a matter of fact, I do,” she said, lifting her chin.

“Easy now, girl. Can’t a man ask a question in his own country?”

Abruptly, she pushed back her chair. “I’m very tired. I think I’ll go to bed.” She did not look at him as she carried her dishes over to the sink. “Thank you for the meal. I really appreciate it.”

“Not a bother,” he said, standing up quickly, the chair scraping against the floor. “If you need anything, let me know. I’m down the hall.”

She nodded, bid him good night, and disappeared. He stood there a moment, staring at the empty space she left behind.

RUTH CLOSED the door behind her and leaned against it. Rain pelted against the window. Here she was in the middle of nowhere with a landlord who always seemed to be laughing at her. Well, she’d be gone by tomorrow, which was just as well. He wasn’t the first person to be condescending when he found out she wrote romance for a living, but it always got on her nerves.

She had no choice but to wear her clean clothes to bed. Her nightgowns and pajamas were in the luggage that was somewhere between New York and Ireland. She climbed into the big bed with the many covers and burrowed underneath them. When her head sank back into the pillow, she sighed. Exhaustion began to lull her to sleep, but she was soon interrupted by a knock on her door.

Sitting up, she pulled the blankets to her chest. "Who is it?" she called out. She rolled her eyes as soon as the words were out of her mouth.

"Take a wild guess," Sean said from the other side of the door.

"What is it?" she asked, leery of him. Had there been a lock on the door, she would have used it before getting into bed, but there was none. What kind of establishment had no locks on the guest-room doors?

"I wondered if you would like a jar?" Sean asked.

Sighing, she climbed out of the bed and opened the door a crack, peering at him.

"A what?"

He held up a fleece-covered hot water bottle.

She frowned at it.

"May I come in?" he asked.

Ruth hesitated, then opened the door wider to allow him entrance.

Without further ado, he walked into her room, lifted up the flat sheet and the blankets at the foot of the bed, slid the hot water bottle underneath them, and then tucked everything back in.

"There, now put your feet down there," he said.

Ruth climbed back in and stretched her legs out, and her feet landed on the warm and toasty fleece.

"Oh. That's very nice," she said, resting her feet on the 'jar.' "Thank you."

Sean chuckled and headed toward the door.

"Sean?"

He turned to look at her.

"Why are there no locks on the doors?"

"I took them off last year," he explained. "My brother's lads kept locking each other in the rooms, and I got tired of pulling the ladder out and climbing through the windows. Good night, Ruth Davenport." He left the room and softly shut the door behind him.

Ruth stared after him for a long time before she finally fell asleep.

As Sean headed back to the kitchen, he pulled his phone out of his pocket and typed Ruth's name into the Amazon search bar. Immediately, a list of her books popped up. He studied the covers: the happy faces of embracing couples against pastel-colored backdrops. He shook his head. The thought of making a living giving people false hope, now that was something. Fair play to her, he thought. He clicked on her name and studied her official author photo. Her red hair was piled on top of her head and she was smiling, with the light from a setting sun streaming around her. She was very pretty.

From the back room, he heard the washing machine buzz, signaling the end of the cycle. Turning his phone off, he went to retrieve the wash. He pulled out his guest's frock, smiling at the explosion of flowers on the fabric. Very feminine. He pulled the air dryer out, took both items back to the kitchen, and set the dryer up in front of the range. Carefully, he laid her dress out on the dryer, noting the rip along the seam. He fingered it thoughtfully. His mother's old sewing kit was around somewhere, and after a search, he located it at the back of one of the presses in the kitchen. He sat down in his chair, put his legs up on the table, and threaded a needle. Focusing, he turned the dress inside out and went to work on repairing the seam.

He looked to the dog, who had settled at his feet. "She hasn't even been here that long and she's already causing trouble. That's a woman for you."

The dog ignored him and laid his head down, closing his eyes.

# CHAPTER EIGHT

When Ruth opened her eyes the following morning and took in the faded floral wallpaper and the sun shining through the white net curtains, it took her a moment to remember where she was and how she got there.

She sat up, noting she already felt much better than she had the previous night. Sinking back down among the blankets, she yawned and stretched before gathering the blankets up around her shoulder.

The room, though dated, was charming. And it was clean. The bed had been so comfortable that eventually, despite being troubled by the events of the evening and the enigmatic landlord, she caved in to sleep. And when it finally came, it was solid.

Energized, she threw back the covers and sat on the edge of the bed.

She was relieved to find that her leg didn't ache at all, despite all the problems yesterday. She stood on her tiptoes, stretching and yawning again. The sunshine beckoned her, and she stepped over to the window and pulled the lace curtain to one side.

"Oh," she said when she saw the black-and-white cows in the back pasture. The grass was still dewy from all the rain the night before, but the cows munched lazily, their tails swishing. It was a sight that calmed Ruth; it was one she could easily get used to.

After a while, she turned from the window and made the bed, then went through her carry-on to find her hairbrush and toothbrush.

Retrieving both, she walked softly to the door, opened it, and peered out. The hallway was quiet, and she could see that the bathroom was unoccupied.

As quietly as she could, she walked down the hall toward the bathroom. All was silent, and she figured that Sean was still in bed. Running a pub, he probably didn't get up too early. She couldn't blame him for sleeping in if he kept late nights.

She had just reached the threshold of the bathroom when a voice from behind her boomed, "Good morning, Ruth Davenport."

Ruth jumped, dropping her hairbrush and toothbrush.

"You're a pile of nerves," Sean said.

She bent over to pick up her lost items and heard him chuckle behind her. Probably at her backside, which she'd more or less just offered to him. Quickly, she stood up. Over her shoulder, she shot him a glance. Once again, he appeared to be laughing at her.

"Just enjoying the view," he said, rubbing his beard.

Without a word, she went into the bathroom and closed the door firmly behind her. She didn't want to slam it; after all, he had put her up for the night.

Once she finished her morning ablutions, she headed out to the kitchen. Sean stood at the stove, stirring something around in a cast-iron frying pan.

"Do ye fancy a bit of breakfast?" he asked. He was no longer laughing, and she relaxed a bit. She had to admit that she was starving. But then, she was always hungry.

She nodded.

"Be ready in five minutes," he said, turning his attention back to the pan.

She dug through her purse for the airport man's

card. She tried dialing her cell phone but the battery was dead. "Ugh," she groaned.

Sean glanced at her and gestured, spatula in hand, toward the phone in the hallway. "You can use the landline."

"Thank you," she said. Taking the business card, she went out to the hall and dialed the number. The man who had helped her the day before was not there, she was told, so she had to go through her spiel again about her lost luggage. The man at the other end asked for an address where they could reach her.

"Hold on one minute," she said, and placed the phone down. Standing in the doorframe of the kitchen, she was momentarily distracted by all the smells of a cooking breakfast. Her mouth watered.

She looked up to Sean. "Is it all right if I have my luggage delivered here? I mean, when they find it."

He looked up from the fry pan with a hint of mischief around his eyes. "So ye plan on staying then?"

She paused, not wanting to impose. "Would it be all right if I stayed just until my luggage is delivered? Then I'll be out of your hair."

"Fair enough," he said.

"What is the address here?" she asked.

"The Town Pub, The Square, Ballybeg, County Tipperary," he answered.

She frowned. "Is that it?"

Sean nodded. "Yes." He pulled two plates down from a rack on the wall.

"It seems like there should be some numbers," she said.

"Sorry."

"No zip code?" she asked. Somehow the address didn't seem complete without a zip code.

"It's grand; it'll get here." He winked. "We're the only pub in Ballybeg."

Ruth didn't want to add that they were the only anything in the village.

She rattled off the address to the man at the airport, then hung up the phone and felt a small sense of accomplishment.

There was a steaming pot of tea in the center of the table, and Ruth took it upon herself to pour some into the two waiting mugs while Sean plated up their breakfast. He had laid out slices of toast in a rack, and there was fresh butter and orange marmalade. Ruth was impressed: he set a nice table.

She noticed her dress on the clothes dryer and went over to inspect it, wondering if the tear could be fixed. It had cleaned up well and dried nicely, as had the lavender cardigan she'd worn with it.

She fingered the dress, frowning. The tear on the side of the skirt portion of the dress had been mended. She looked over to Sean, who had been watching her. He shrugged and said casually, "I was bored last night, so I mended your frock."

"Wow. Thank you," she said.

He gave a slight bow and said, "You're welcome." He laid down the two plates of breakfast, and Ruth's eyes widened at her heaping plate. There were two eggs over easy, sausages, rashers, beans, and four discs: two white and two black. Some kind of sausage, Ruth surmised.

She pulled out a chair across the table from him, sat down, and dug into her breakfast.

"Did they say what day they'd drop off your luggage?" Sean asked, buttering his toast.

Ruth looked up from her plate. Her brows knitted together. "No, I just assumed it would be today." When he didn't say anything, she said, "You don't think they'd drop it off today?"

He shook his head. "I think they'll drop it off when they get around to it."

"Well, I have no clothes. This is it," she said, gesturing to what she had on and the floral dress hanging on the clothes rack.

He raised his eyebrows and grinned. "What more do you need?"

She was about to say something about clean underwear, but with his grin, she decided otherwise.

"Would there be a store in town where I could pick up some things, like clothing?"

He shook his head. "Nah, two villages over."

"I would like to get to my car today and see what I need to do with that, as well," she added.

She looked pointedly at him, but he wouldn't look at her. Finally, he sighed. "Yes, I'll take you to your car and to a shop to pick up some bits until your luggage arrives."

"Thank you, I'll pay you for your time," she said.

He didn't say anything, just poured more tea into his mug.

"What kind of sausage is this?" she asked, mopping up her egg with a piece of toast. "It's delicious." Only half of one of the four disks was left on her plate. She glanced over to the pan to see if there were any more.

Sean smiled. "It's black and white pudding. Made from pig's blood."

~

AFTER BREAKFAST, Sean and Ruth went out to his car. She was able to get a better look at her surroundings in the broad daylight. Ballybeg was a sleepy, rural village with a post office, the pub, a small food shop, and a church. A modest crowd streamed out of the church after morning Mass and headed toward the shop. Ruth watched them with interest.

"Hop in, Ruth Davenport," Sean said. He waved to some of the villagers.

Once she was settled into the passenger seat, he turned to her and asked, "Do you remember where you crashed your car?"

"Yes, I do, up that road," she said, pointing straight ahead. "I know I came into the village from that direction, because the pub was on my right."

Sean threw the car in gear and pulled out of the paved carpark of the pub. He looked both ways and proceeded up the hill. It wasn't long before he noticed the muddy tire tracks off the side of the road, the low, clipped hedge, and the gash in the great oak tree in the field. He cast a glance at Ruth and saw by the expression on her face that she hadn't noticed what he had noticed. Yet. Her rental car was no longer there.

*Five, four, three—* he thought to himself.

"Hey, wait a minute," Ruth said, indignant. "I left my car right there, against that tree."

He didn't argue with her that she hadn't 'left' it

there; she had crashed it there. Sean pulled over from the road as far as he could without sliding into the ditch. They both got out of the car, and she stood with her mouth open, both hands on her hips.

"I don't understand. I left it right there!" she said. She looked up and down the road, then back to Sean.

"Well, it must be around here somewhere," he said. Of all the fields she could crash her car into, it had to be this one. He twirled the toothpick in his mouth, wondering how to go about this.

Ruth laid her hand against her forehead, sweeping her hair back. "I don't believe this!"

"It'll turn up," he said optimistically.

"It can't be stolen!" she said. "Who would steal a wrecked car?"

"Well, they'd steal it for the scrap metal," he said.

She frowned at him. "That is not helpful."

He tried a different tact. "Technically, we don't know that it's stolen. You've just misplaced it."

He could see her getting frustrated.

"I haven't misplaced it," she insisted.

He cocked an eyebrow. "Do you know where your car is?"

"No," she conceded.

"Then you've misplaced it," he said.

She rolled her eyes.

"Look, let's go on to the shops," he said. He couldn't spend all day driving her around; he did have a business to run. "When we come back, we can make inquiries."

"Maybe we should call the police," she said. "Or maybe we should contact the owner of this field. He might know."

Sean looked at her. That was the last thing he was going to do: contact the present owner of the field.

# CHAPTER NINE

Ruth worried about her car. It was bad enough that she'd crashed it and had no ground transportation, but now she couldn't even locate it. How was she going to explain that to the rental company?

"Is there bus or train service?" she asked, looking over at Sean. His skin was fair and his hair as dark as a black, inky night.

"Need a set of wheels now, do you?"

"Well, I have some traveling to do around the country while I'm here," she explained. She fidgeted in her seat. Her trip had definitely not gotten off to a good start. Thinking out loud, she said, "Maybe I could hire a driver."

Sean took his eyes off the road momentarily and

looked at her. “How long do you plan on staying, and where do you have to go?”

“I’m here for six weeks. I need to go to Killarney, Dublin, and Cork,” she said.

“Does the time matter?” he asked.

“Mostly daytime,” she said.

He stared out the windshield, his expression hard to read. “Leave it with me. I might have an idea.”

~

SEAN HADN’T BEEN EXAGGERATING when he said the dress shops were two villages over. They stayed on the main route, driving through open countryside until they came to the first village, then again through more countryside until they arrived at the second. Ruth gazed out the window at the scenery. Everything was so green and hilly. Wild yellow gorse grew sporadically along the hillside, and there was a small scattering of houses. Black-and-white cows lazed along the hills.

Ruth wasn’t long in the town. After purchasing some toiletries of a more feminine variety and a few dresses, she headed toward the carpark where she had left Sean chewing on a toothpick and reading a newspaper.

He folded up the paper and threw it in the backseat as she approached. "Did you get all your bits and bobs?"

"I did."

"Then let's get a move on; I've got a pub to open."

"Why do you chew on the toothpicks?" she asked.

"I started when I quit smoking."

"How long ago was that?"

He looked up to one side, thinking. "Huh. Almost twenty years ago since I gave up the fags."

Ruth did some quick math in her head, and her eyes widened. "How old were you when you started smoking?"

He looked at her evenly. "Twelve."

"You were smoking at twelve?" she asked in disbelief.

He shrugged as if it were nothing. "I grew up in a pub, and it seemed the thing to do."

"Aren't you afraid of swallowing a toothpick?" she asked, intrigued.

He nodded. "As a matter of fact, I have swallowed a few bits and pieces over the last two decades." He paused, then added, "I'm probably three toothpicks short of a picket fence."

Ruth laughed. "You're a funny one, Sean

Hughes."

She looked at him. Sean Hughes was smiling at her. Not his usual cheeky grin, but the first genuine smile she'd seen from him.

~

SEAN HAD NOT BEEN able to concentrate on the paper while the American had been shopping. Her problems could be the solution to his own. They were both in a jam. She needed transportation for her six-week stay, and he needed some cash to get that boiler fixed before winter.

As they headed back to the pub, they rode in silence for a bit before he remarked casually, "You know, Ruth Davenport, I think we may be able to help each other out."

He looked over at her in the passenger seat. She was a very pretty girl, but she seemed a bit uptight. He wondered if she was high maintenance.

"Ruth?" he asked, breaking her reverie.

"Yes?" she asked, giving her head a slight shake.

"Well, you're looking for a driver to get you around the country to do your research, and I could use a bit of extra cash," he said bluntly. "Here's my proposal: I'll drive you around the country and provide you with accommodation and all your meals in return for a flat fee. Fifty percent down and fifty percent when you leave. I'll also supply the petrol."

She bit her lip, turned, and stared out the window. They'd driven a few miles before she spoke.

"Any stipulations?" she finally asked.

"I'd only ask that you book your appointments in the mornings or early afternoons, because I have to be back to open the pub. Marie could pinch hit a few times, but I can't ask her to do that every day. But Mondays are my days off, so they're wide open."

"I wouldn't want to ruin your day off," she said. She looked up at him from under her long, dark lashes.

*Yes, she is pretty. Keep on moving, son, nothing to see here.*

"What do you usually do on your day off?" she asked.

He shrugged again, hesitant to disclose his private life. How would he explain that he did nothing? That he liked to hang out with his dog and read poetry? *Oh my God, I've turned into the male version of a cat lady.*

"I'm sorry, I didn't mean to pry," she said.

"No, not at all," he said. What did it matter what she thought of him? After six weeks, he'd never see her again. "Actually, if the weather is nice, I take a book and Shep up to a nice spot and enjoy the view, the company of my dog, and a good read."

"Is there tea?" she asked.

"Yes, of course," he replied, surprised at her question.

"It sounds heavenly," she said quietly.

As they drove back, Ruth's phone rang and she answered it, and after a moment her face broke into a broad smile. She turned to Sean. "They've found my luggage!" She thanked the airport official profusely.

"You should smile more often. It suits you," Sean noted.

From her side of the car, Ruth blushed.

RUTH'S LUGGAGE arrived at the pub before she did. Unfortunately, the suitcase was wide open, with her personal belongings scattered across the asphalt.

Horrified, Ruth looked at the sight of her clothes, including her lacy bras and underwear, strewn all over the place.

"I see the airline has dropped off your luggage," Sean observed, working the toothpick in his mouth.

"'Dropped' being the key word," Ruth said.

"I always did want to put flowers out front," Sean remarked, his eyes following the trail of floral panties, nightgowns, and dresses.

"I like flowers," she said defensively.

"You don't say," he said with the hint of a smile.

Sean hadn't even put the car into park when Ruth jumped out, laying her hands on her head in dismay. Despite the sunny day, there had been a slight breeze and as a result, Ruth's clothes were everywhere: dresses, cardigans, and everything else hanging off flower pots, snagged on the hedge of the adjoining field, and littering the small parking lot. Hurriedly, she began snatching up items of clothing, clutching them with one hand to her chest and using her free hand to gather the rest.

In horror, she watched as Sean unsnagged a floral lace brassiere from the bench of one of the picnic tables. He grinned as he looped the strap around his finger. Quickly, she grabbed it from him and shoved it to the bottom of her suitcase. Ruth thought of every hero she had ever written about, and the consensus was that none of them would have used the present situation to have a laugh.

As fast as she could, she pulled the rest of her things together, shoving everything into the suitcase in one big, crumpled mess. Once finished, she planted her hands on her hips and surveyed the area to see if she had missed anything. Sean had the packet of her letters from the Clonmel Marriage Bureau in his hands. He stared at the top letter, a smile beginning to form on his face.

Ruth marched over as quickly as her leg would allow to retrieve her personal correspondence, but not quick enough to keep Sean from spotting the return address on the top envelope.

"What's this? The Clonmel Marriage Bureau?" he asked. Now he was laughing. And Ruth felt like crying.

"Those are personal if you don't mind," she said, her eyes narrowing and her voice shaking. There were boundaries, and she felt as if her privacy had been invaded.

He cocked an eyebrow and grinned. "Oh, I don't mind."

He didn't resist when she grabbed the bundle out of his hand. Turning on her heel, she shoved the letters into her suitcase underneath the pile of clothes.

"Research, my arse," he said behind her.

She pulled up short and gritted her teeth, but chose to ignore him. It didn't warrant a response. He probably thought she was just another desperate female in search of love. To try and correct him would be futile.

Satisfied and relieved that everything was back in the suitcase, she zipped it up.

Without a word, Sean picked up her suitcase and carried it inside. He was still grinning. She let him carry it without protesting, as penance for laughing at her.

Suddenly, she felt weary. Nothing had gone right since she'd stepped off the plane. And there didn't seem to be any improvement coming. Maybe coming here had been a mistake. In the past, she'd always used the internet for research. She could have done the same for this next book.

Outside the door of her room, Sean set her suitcase down and looked at her. His voice, soft and lilting, broke through her thoughts. "I recognize that look."

Crossing her arms across her chest, she regarded him sharply and began to wonder if she was that easy to read. She seriously hoped not; she liked to retain some mystery about her.

He said softly, "You look like you're in desperate need of a cup of tea."

She looked away.

He smiled. "Come on, then, I'll put the kettle on."

~

SEAN DIDN'T KNOW what to think about the pretty redhead writing to this Clonmel Marriage Bureau. Some people just had marriage on their minds. He would like to have warned them that it wasn't all it was cracked up to be. At the end of the day, you still had two people with their own agendas.

"Tell me, Ruth, do you have a fella back home?" he asked, pushing his teacup away.

Ruth squirmed in her seat. "No, I don't."

"Is that why you're writing to the marriage bureau?"

She tilted her head. "It's a little far to go for a date, don't you think?"

He laughed. "That it is."

"After five books, I was stuck for something to write about when I came across this article for the Clonmel agency, and it was just the sort of inspiration I needed," she explained.

"So you signed up in the name of research?" he asked, curious.

Ruth shook her head. "No, I didn't sign up. I contacted the woman who runs the agency and was upfront about my intent to gather research for my next book.

"Any takers?" he asked.

She nodded. "Three. They've been quite helpful."

"And do they know you're only in it for the research?"

"Yes."

One look at her—that hair, those eyes, that figure—and the men of Ireland would want to do a lot more than help her with her research.

"And what if one of them thinks there's a chance for romance?" he asked.

"They can't be serious about a relationship with someone three thousand miles away," she protested.

"You'd be surprised what people can be serious about," he said. After Brid had run off to Dublin, he had hoped they would continue their relationship long distance, and Dublin was a lot closer than New York. But she had wanted an indefinite break. A break that was now going on for over three years.

His guest went quiet, and he wondered what she was thinking. Even if it was inadvertent, it was typical to get a man's hopes up and then break his heart. Was this a universal thing among women?

"I've arranged to meet them to interview them," Ruth explained.

"And what if they should fall for you? Is it worth breaking their hearts in the name of research?" he asked.

"I highly doubt anyone will fall in love with me on a first date," she said with an incredulous laugh.

Sean frowned. "Why not?"

"I would think once they saw my leg, they would not be interested," she said.

Bending down, he lifted the tablecloth and peeked at her legs beneath the table. He thought they were a fine pair of legs. Quickly, she bent them underneath her chair, removing them from his view.

Sitting up straight, he asked, "What's wrong with your leg?"

"You're joking, right?" she asked.

He shook his head.

"You've seen that I walk with a limp."

His eyebrows knitted together. "What does that have to do with anything?"

Suddenly, she stood up from the table. "I need to do some work. Do you have Wi-Fi here?" She would not make eye contact with him.

He didn't understand. "What's wrong? What did I say?"

She turned her gaze toward him, folding her arms across her chest. "Really? Now you're going to play dumb?"

He tried a grin. "Sometimes I'm not playing."

She sighed and closed her eyes. "Is everything funny to you?"

"Sometimes. Anyway, my question."

"Really? My leg. My limp. There are men out there that would automatically discount me because of it."

"Really?" He knew some people were shallow, but this?

"Yes, really."

"Has a man ever told you he didn't want to take you out because of your limp?" he asked. Now he was interested.

Without hesitation, she replied, "Yes."

"What kind of people have you been palling around with?"

"To a lot of people, appearances mean something," she said.

"But a limp? Look, where I come from, and you can see where I come from,"—he waved his hand around for effect— "that sort of thing doesn't matter."

The expression on her face said she was not convinced.

He spoke in a rush. "Look at Maeve and Dennis at the top of the village. He lost his arm in a farming accident. Maeve didn't leave him."

"But she was already with him when the accident happened," Ruth argued.

Sean shook his head. He wasn't buying this.

Yes, men were visual creatures, but to him, there was so much more than just looks. "Just last week, they had an article in the paper about a solicitor who found love after a paragliding accident left him paralyzed from the neck down."

"Look, I really do need to get some writing done," she said. "Is there Wi-Fi in the bar?"

"Yes, but wouldn't you rather write up here where it's quiet?" he asked. He stuffed his hands in his pockets.

"Actually, no. At home, I write in the kitchen, where my father always has the TV on," she explained. "Sometimes I go down to the local coffee shop and write there." She paused. "Unless of course, you don't want me working down in the pub."

"Of course not."

As she headed out the door, he called after her, "Did you think any more about my offer?"

"All right. We'll sort out the details later," she called back.

He threw a fist pump into the air. It wouldn't cover the complete cost of the boiler, but it would help. He wouldn't have to use all his savings, and his plan to purchase more fruit trees in the next year was still achievable.

# CHAPTER TEN

From a little booth in the corner of the Off the Beaten Track pub, Ruth had a clear view of the bar across the room. Her laptop open in front of her, she was working on character analyses of her two main characters. But at the same time, one of her favorite pastimes was observing people, and here she could get a sense of the local community.

The first thing she took away was that they all knew one another and spent some considerable amount of time together, judging by the way they bantered back and forth and teased one another. The second thing she deduced was that they were a very friendly bunch and went out of their way to make her feel welcome.

"Safe travels, lass," said one old fella.

Another woman, not too much older than Ruth, gushed about how much she loved New York City, the shopping, and going out for breakfast.

As unobtrusively as possible, Ruth watched Sean work his trade and concluded that he was a born publican. He gave as good as he got. Ruth was curious about the relationship he had with the old man in the brown tweed cap at the far end of the bar. He was a little man, no more than five four, and he sat hunched over his pint as if it were the most precious thing in the world to him. Sean would walk over to him, lean over the bar, and the two would share snippets of conversation. The old man must have been funny because more than once, Sean walked away laughing and shaking his head. What moved Ruth was how solicitous he was toward the old man, even serving him a ham sandwich with a small bowl of soup at one point.

Ruth leaned back against the low upholstered booth, resting her palms on the seat. When she looked up, she caught Sean looking at her. He smiled and she blushed, looking away.

He sauntered over to the table, picking up empty draft bottles and glasses on the way.

"Would you have something to drink?" he asked.

She shook her head. "No, thank you."

"Suit yourself," he said, ambling back to the bar.

Even though she preferred clean-shaven, his look was starting to grow on her. So decidedly Irish with his dark hair, fair skin, and blue eyes. He was tall, well over six foot, but he was lean, one of those people who could eat whatever they wanted and not gain a pound. Although she herself was tall for a woman at almost five nine, she was solid. Always had been. There was nothing delicate about her. Until the car accident, and then she'd discovered how fragile her leg was.

MUCH LATER, Ruth went up to the bar to get some more water. Secretly, she hoped Sean would serve her last so she could observe him up close. She had pub patrons to her left and right. There were a couple of farmers and the old man who sat in the corner leaning against the wall. To her right were the undertaker, Calvin, and the postman, Moss. It did not go unnoticed by Ruth that Calvin seemed quite smitten with Marie. In fact, on observation, it appeared that everyone was aware of Calvin's obvious infatuation. Everyone, that is, except Marie herself.

"I've heard you already managed to bang up your car," Marie said, taking Ruth's empty glass.

Ruth grimaced in response. "Unfortunately, that is correct."

"Will you have to get another one?" Marie asked, replacing her glass with a fresh drink.

Ruth shook her head. Sean stepped closer.

"No, didn't Sean tell you? We've come to an agreement, and he's going to give me rides all over the country," Ruth explained.

There was immediate silence around her. The expression on Sean's face froze, and Marie appeared grim-faced. The man to Ruth's right said, "Oh, I'll bet Sean's going to give you a ride." That broke the silence, and laughter ensued.

Someone yelled, "I'll give you a ride if that's what you're after." More laughter. Even the old man in the corner was laughing; Ruth could tell by the shaking of his shoulders.

Ruth frowned, uncomprehending.

Sean walked away and with a glance over his shoulder, called out to her, "Ruth, would you come here to me?"

Ruth followed him to the other end of the bar.

Sean leaned over the bar and whispered, "You

might want to tell people that I'm giving you a lift instead."

"Why?" Ruth asked, beginning to think they were a peculiar lot.

Sean emitted a "what am I going to do with her" sigh. "The verb 'ride' has a different context here."

She shook her head, not following.

"Well," he stammered. "I'm a man, and you're a woman."

"Well done, Sean, for figuring that out," Ruth joked.

He rewarded her with a smile and leaned across the bar to her. She was so close to him she could just about reach out and touch his beard. She'd like to touch it.

Lowering his voice, he said, "Here, if a man fancies a woman, he might want to ride her." He twirled the toothpick in his mouth and watched her intently.

Ruth jumped back as if burned. Her hands flew to her face.

"Oh," she said.

Sean raised his eyebrows slightly, stared at her, and smiled.

Her own eyes widened, and she said a little louder, "Oh!"

He headed back to the bar. Ruth resumed her

position at the bar and said loudly, "Just to clarify, Sean Hughes has offered to give me a lift." There, she'd said it. "A lift, that's all."

"But it probably won't be long before he's offering to give you a ride," someone said.

More laughter. Ruth threw up her hands and announced, "I give up." This made them laugh harder. Retreating to the safety of the corner booth, Ruth kept a low profile for the rest of the evening.

THE FOLLOWING MORNING, Sean decided he could put it off no longer. It wasn't fair to Ruth to keep her from searching for her rental car, especially when he had a very good idea where it was likely to be. Sometimes he wished he were a drinking man. Because right then, he could use a stiff drink. Preferably whiskey. They'd have to go to the McGonagle house, the family home of Bridget "Brid" McGonagle, his former fiancée. There had been rumors in the village that she had returned from Dublin. If she had, she had not shown up at the pub. She probably hadn't expected him to wait for her all these years. But somehow, he had. Either he was a romantic or a fool. Most likely the latter.

Ruth entered the kitchen wearing a dress with a

white background and splashes of pink roses. She'd paired it with a pink cardigan.

"I suppose we should talk to the farmer who owns the field where your rental car was last seen," he said casually. He poured steaming tea from a pot into the two mugs laid out on the table.

"Good idea," she replied.

He stood up from the table and went to the stove to cook her a fry-up.

"You don't have to go to all that trouble for breakfast," she said. She eyed the plate of scones and jar of jam on the table. "A scone is fine for me."

"Are you sure?" he asked, unconvinced. "We can't have you passing out because you're weak with the hunger."

She shook her head. "No, really, tea and a scone will be fine."

He was surprised at his disappointment. He would have liked to cook her breakfast again. She had a good appetite and there was nothing more enjoyable than cooking for someone who enjoyed eating.

Still, despite refusing a hot breakfast, she managed to polish off two raisin scones with liberal amounts of butter and jam, and two hot cups of tea.

~

On the drive over to the McGonagle farm, Sean didn't say much. Figuring he'd go right to the top, he prayed to the three patron saints of Ireland—Patrick, Brigid, and Columba—that Brid wouldn't answer the door. But any apprehension he held about the meeting soon dissolved with the distraction of the American in the passenger seat, who chattered merrily, making observations on the way over.

"I noticed there aren't really any road markings or signs," she said. "It's amazing you're able to find anything at all."

"We've all been around here for so long, we just know where everything is," he answered, at a loss for an explanation himself. "If you take that road past the pub by the big crooked tree, that's the Dublin road."

Ruth frowned. "Why's it called the Dublin road?"

"Because if you stay on it, it will take you to Dublin," he explained.

"Oh, of course," she said. "And what if you take the road in the opposite direction?"

"That's the Limerick road," he replied.

She nodded. "Because that will take you to Limerick."

Having lived there his whole life, he knew all the roads and where they led to. He knew the big two-story house at the bad bend in the road, and the family that had lived there for generations. There was the Bridge of Tears over the small river just outside the village, where historically, people who left Ireland congregated before catching the stage-coach to the shore, which would take them to the docks and the ships that would take them to far-flung places all over the world: America, Canada, and Australia, to name a few.

There were no street names in rural Ireland, but the houses had names. It was just the way it was. His uncle's farmhouse was Roseview Cottage, after Mackie's mother's beloved rose garden, which was still in evidence to the present day.

Before he knew it, they were turning onto the drive that led to the McGonagle farmhouse. Grass grew in the middle of the verge. In the front of the big two-story building were huge oak and sycamore trees that had been there longer than the house. Barns and whitewashed stone buildings sat to the right. Sean eyed up the herd of black-and-white dairy cows in the front pasture. In a few weeks the weather would worsen, getting darker, colder, and rainier, and the bovine population would be taken inside to the barns for the winter.

It had been a long time since he'd been there. The last time had been three weeks before their planned wedding. Brid had told him that she wasn't sure, that she needed a break. That she needed to get away to do one last thing before she settled down. She left, headed off to Dublin, and last he'd heard she was working at RTE, the national broadcaster. At first, he'd been devastated. But then he figured she'd get it out of her system and be back home to him in six weeks. After a year passed with no word from her, he realized she might come back home, but she wouldn't be coming back to him. As Ruth chattered on, he was surprised to find that those old feelings of anger and hurt were no longer there. It confused him. He had just assumed that they would be his companions for the rest of his life.

"Look, there's my car," Ruth said excitedly. But her excitement soon abated when she saw the condition of the rental, with the front of it looking like an accordion.

"I take it it was in better condition when you picked it up from the airport," Sean remarked.

"What am I going to do?" she wailed.

"Did you get the collision insurance?" he asked.

“I did, but there’s a deductible,” she said. “Well, at least it’s not stolen, because I didn’t get that type of insurance.”

He smiled as he pulled the car in front of the house and shifted it into park. “Well, at least there is that.”

They climbed out of the car and Sean stared at the front door, deciding it was time to confront his past.

# CHAPTER ELEVEN

Sean and Ruth stood next to each other on the doorstep of Brid's family home. The front door was painted an enameled red. Sean had given a good rap on it and they waited, silent.

Before the door opened, there was a shout from inside. "Who's there?"

Sean rolled his eyes. Mr. McGonagle. It cheered him to no end that he was still as pleasant as he used to be.

The door swung open and Brid's father stood there, wearing a navy pullover and brown corduroy pants. His hair was gray, and his eyebrows stood out prominently. He peered at them.

"Who is it?" he demanded.

Sean cleared his throat. "Mr. McGonagle, it's me, Sean Hughes."

"Oh, is it now?" the man said with a smile, but it wasn't a friendly one. "I suppose you heard my Brid was home and thought you better get over here to stake your claim. Well, I said it before and I'll say it again: you were never good enough for her!"

Sean seethed. Out of respect for the man's age, he bit his tongue. "Actually, I'm not here to see Brid." He looked over at Ruth, who had just witnessed a dose of Irish hospitality at its finest. "I'm here about the car that landed in your field."

Ruth spoke up. "I slid off the road the other night in the rain. I'm so relieved to have found it."

"Young lady, you've done a lot of damage to my field."

"I-I am truly sorry about that, sir," she stammered.

"As you should be!" he said. He glanced over at Sean. "I see you're still chewing on that toothpick. Honest to God, I don't know what my Brid ever saw in you."

Ignoring the man's rudeness, Sean said, "Can we get the car?"

"No, you can't," Mr. McGonagle replied. "It's not drivable."

"But it's a rental car, and I need to return it," Ruth said.

"Not my problem, miss," he said, and went to close the door.

Sean blocked it with his foot. "Look, we just want to get the car and then we'll be on our way."

"No!" the man said. "Now remove your foot from my doorstep and yourselves from my farm."

Sean took a step back, sighing. Brid's father had always been difficult; it was his nature. Obviously, age had not mellowed him.

The door slammed shut and Sean realized one thing: he was glad that Mr. McGonagle wasn't his father-in-law.

Ruth's eyes had welled up and her face had gone red.

"Hey, come on," he said, reaching out to her but then pulling his hand away. "Don't cry."

"But my car, I have to turn it in when I leave," she said. "I can't leave it here."

"Come on, let's go," he said. He clamped his teeth down on his toothpick.

She hesitated, and he indicated with a nod of his head that she was to follow him. "Leave it with me, Ruth." He muttered under his breath, "There's more than one way to skin a cat."

~

Once the details of their arrangement were sorted out between Sean and Ruth, she gave him his fifty percent deposit in cash. She also notified the Clonmel Marriage Bureau of her temporary address for the next few weeks. Workwise, she had completed her character analyses and done a basic plot outline. Further development of the outline would happen over time. Sometimes, she had to let an idea simmer for a bit to see what would turn up. She was hopeful that her interviews with the people from the marriage bureau would inspire her.

In the meantime, she'd made arrangements to meet one of her pen pals. Her first stop was Killarney, to meet Declan. What she knew from his letters was that he was a farmer with sheep and dairy cows. His picture showed him to be reasonably handsome, with sandy hair and brown eyes in a round face. He looked kind, she'd decided.

On the agreed-upon date, Ruth and Sean drove away from County Tipperary, passing through villages with names like Mitchelstown, Castletownroche, and Mallow in Cork County. She was entranced by the long sloping valleys of the Irish countryside, and the fields that were rich and green even at the end of September. Signs for smaller villages with names like Ballyhooley and New Twopothouse intrigued her, and she wished she had time to explore these places. She mused about how it would sound to say, "I went to New Twopothouse village today."

"What is the plan?" Sean asked, startling her from her reverie.

"Um, well, I'm meeting someone to gather information for the book I'm writing," she explained. Best to keep it simple, she thought.

"And the information revolves around this marriage bureau?" he asked.

*He would ask that*, she thought. "Yes."

He shook his head. "Are there no dating agencies in the US? It seems a long way to travel just for research."

"There are, but this one is more traditional. The letter writing inspires me." She paused and added, "Besides, the book is set in Ireland. So I'm interested in the people and culture of Ireland as well as the marriage bureau."

"Do you like writing letters yourself, Ruth? Receiving them?"

She felt his eyes on her and wished he'd keep them on the road. His scrutiny caused her to shift in her seat. "Both, actually."

"Tell me, what will you do if one of these men expresses a romantic interest in you?"

Ruth shrugged. "As I've said before, I really don't see that happening. I've made it clear that I'm here for research." She regarded him evenly and asked, "Why are you concerned about this?"

It was his turn to shrug. "Just don't want to see one of my fellow Irishmen get hurt."

Ruth leaned back against the door and scrutinized him, eyes narrowed. "Where is this concern coming from? Personal experience?"

"Maybe."

"Anything to do with Brid?" she asked.

He glanced sharply toward her. "That is not a subject for discussion."

A stony silence fell between them and Ruth thought, *Well, this is fun.*

"Why do you write romance?" he asked.

Ruth stared out the window. "I'm good at it, and I like romance."

"Are you having any right now in your life?" he asked.

"I beg your pardon?" she asked, a flush creeping into her cheeks.

"Cool down," he said, his face softening into a smile. "I was talking about romance. What did you think I was talking about?" When no answer was forthcoming, he laughed. “Maybe you’re writing the wrong genre.”

Embarrassed, she said, “Not that it’s any of your business, but no, there is no romance in my life.”

He shifted gears and steered into a turn. “I just want to make sure no jealous boyfriends show up on my doorstep.”

She snorted. “You don’t have to worry about that.”

She felt Sean’s eyes on her, expecting her to elaborate. She was not going to go into detail about her love life, or lack of one, with a stranger. Deciding silence was called for, she turned her head and stared out the window.

AS THEY WHIZZED past the sign that welcomed them into County Kerry, butterflies flew around Ruth’s stomach like they were on speed. When they arrived in Killarney town, her mouth went dry and her stomach clenched. She crossed her arms across her stomach, hoping the action would quell the discomfort. It was not successful.

“Are you all right?” Sean’s voice broke through her anxious reverie, causing her to jump in her seat.

“Whatever is the matter with you?” he asked.

He looked at her, not comprehending. "If you get your knickers in a twist over a bit of research, then perhaps this isn't the career for you."

"I'm fine," she lied. It had been an impulsive move that night to write to the marriage bureau. Her disappointment with Steve Acola had served as an accelerant. She was pleased with the way her story idea was developing, but now here she was, having to meet and converse with a strange man. At least it was a public meeting spot.

"I hope so," he said, unconvinced.

Ruth distracted herself from her queasy stomach by taking in the town. Compared to many of the towns and villages she had seen since her arrival in Ireland, this one was big and bustling with boutique hotels, shops, and restaurants. It was charming and vibrant. There was a buzz in the air, and Ruth's stomach relaxed. Suddenly, she didn't want to interview anyone, but rather explore this lovely town as a tourist.

Sean parked his car in the carpark behind the Killarney Plaza hotel, and she gathered her purse and her raincoat.

"Do you know which way you're going?" he asked.

She nodded and made a move for the door handle. According to Google, the restaurant was in the hotel. All she had to do was make her way around the front, to the entrance on the main street.

"How long do you think you'll need?" he asked.

"An hour would be good," she said. "What will you do during that time?"

"If you'll only be gone an hour, I'll wait here and read the paper," he said, picking up the folded newspapers that were tucked between the two seats.

Ruth glanced at her watch. "I'll be back in an hour."

She climbed out of the car and looped her purse over her shoulder. Determined, Ruth walked toward the sidewalk that would skirt around to the front of the hotel. She glanced back once. Sean waved to her from the car, and she turned around quickly.

RUTH HAD a general idea of what Declan Mulqueen looked like from the postcard-sized photo he'd sent. The information that came from the marriage bureau had listed his height as five foot two, but Ruth had naturally assumed that that couldn't be right. It must have been a typo; certainly, it should be a six instead of a five. She stood for a few minutes near the bar, scanning the area.

When she felt a nudge at her elbow, she looked

down and saw that the information had been correct: it was supposed to be a five and not a six.

"Is it Ruth?" enquired the man. He appeared older and a little more weather-worn than his picture had led her to believe.

"It is," she said.

"Ye said ye'd be wearing flowers on your frock and by God, woman, you weren't joking," he enthused. He was only a few inches above eye level with her breasts, and from the smile on his face, he appeared to be enjoying the view.

With a smile, she held out her hand and said, "Ruth Davenport, it's nice to meet you, Declan."

"And it's nice to meet you as well," Declan said, wiggling his eyebrows. "Will we sit down?"

"That would be lovely," she replied, wishing she had told Sean she'd be back to the car in half an hour instead of an hour.

"Right this way, I've got us a booth for privacy." He grinned, wiggling his eyebrows again. His eyebrows and their calisthenics were distracting, but in the end, she followed him to a secluded horseshoe booth. She slid into the booth and was a little disconcerted when Declan slid in right beside her. His thigh touched hers, and she moved a few inches away from him. She was relieved to see that sitting down, he was at least eye level with her.

"Would you care for a cocktail?" he asked, looking at her. He wasn't unattractive; he had an open face, and his front teeth were slightly protruding, but not in an ugly manner. Still, she thought a drink was in order.

"I would love one," she answered.

He lifted his hand in the air and snapped his fingers in rapid succession, and Ruth cringed.

"I could just go up to the bar and get a round of drinks," Ruth offered.

Declan shook his head. "You'll do no such thing. That's what the staff here are paid to do." He placed his weathered hand over hers and gave it a protective squeeze.

Not wanting to discuss the finer points of manners and courtesies, Ruth declined comment. As gently as she could, she removed her hand from his and settled it in her lap underneath the table. When the server appeared, looking irritated at the way he'd been summoned, Ruth tried to figure out how to signal an apology.

They ordered a round of drinks, and Declan inched closer to her. "You're more beautiful than your photo, Ruth."

She gave him a slight smile, as she didn't want to encourage him too much. She cleared her throat.

"First, Declan, I want to thank you for agreeing to help me with my research."

He raised an eyebrow and lowered his voice, "It's my pleasure, Ruth." He moved closer to her and as unobtrusively as possible, Ruth inched away. She pulled out a notebook and pen from her purse.

He moved closer again and went to put his arm around her, but she shrugged it off by leaning forward and resting her elbows on the table. "So, you're a farmer. What's that like?"

"Just what you would expect. The farm has been in my family for as long as anyone can remember," he said. "I'm a seventh-generation Mulqueen to farm that land."

"Well, that's impressive."

His eyes narrowing, he said, "We farmers have to be careful who we choose to wed."

"Why's that?" she asked.

"Because sometimes someone gets the notion of marrying a farmer with land, and then before you know it, they're in divorce court, getting half of the farm that's been in a family for generations."

"Yikes," she said, not knowing what else to say.

He chuckled. "Yikes. I like that." The server arrived and set their drinks in front of them.

Once the server left, Ruth lifted her head and

with pen poised, asked, "Declan, can you tell me why you decided to join the marriage bureau?"

"I'm interested in meeting a fine lady," he replied, looking at her pointedly.

"Why the Clonmel Marriage Bureau?"

Looking bored, Declan said, "Because it's old-fashioned. Traditional. And I'm not good on computers, so online dating is out for me."

Ruth nodded, jotting down notes. She tried to get him to talk about his feelings, especially what it was like being a man who lived alone in rural Ireland and was searching for love. But Declan kept changing the subject.

"So, you write books for a living," he remarked.

"I do," Ruth said, pouring the small bottle of tonic water into her glass.

"Is there a good wage in that?" he enquired, sidling up next to her. She inched away again, ignoring his question.

"And it's romance you write?" he asked, sipping his drink.

"It is," she said.

"Don't you find it interesting that you write romance and we're both here?" he asked.

Ruth frowned, not comprehending. They were both there because she was doing research. She'd made that abundantly clear in her letters.

He lowered his voice. “Maybe we could write our own love story. Romeo and Juliet. Bonnie and Clyde.”

Ruth chose not to mention that those couples had not lived happily ever after. She was trying to figure out how to let him down without hurting his feelings. Glancing at her wristwatch, she discovered they’d only been there fifteen minutes. Forty-five to go.

“So where are you staying?” he asked, putting his arm along the back of the upholstered leather booth. That would have been all right if Ruth had wanted it there. But she couldn’t lean back, as his arm would practically be around her. She leaned forward over the table. She also didn’t think it was a good idea to tell him where she was staying. The last thing she needed was anyone showing up unannounced. How on earth would she explain that to Sean?

“My accommodations are varied,” she said. “Never stay in one place more than a night.”

Fingering his cocktail napkin, he looked up at her with a gleam in his eyes. “Ruth Davenport, I have a proposition for you.”

# CHAPTER TWELVE

After Ruth left his car, Sean had given her a few minutes' head start, then trotted after her, following her into the restaurant. Now, from his seat at the hotel bar, he was able to observe everything in the mirror across from him. He sipped at a lemonade as he watched Ruth and that man. Sean told himself that he was only there to make sure everything was aboveboard. But even from his spot twenty feet away, there was no mistaking that the fella had intentions other than helping her with her research. The guy kept edging closer to her and in response, she slid farther away. Sean was no body-language expert, but you wouldn't need to be to know that she wasn't interested in the fella. Sean stiffened and gritted his teeth when the man put his arm around Ruth, but his agitation soon turned to amused interest. She deftly removed the offending arm, and from the expression on her face, Sean suspected she was about to give him a tongue lashing. She was fierce, that one. She edged away from the man again and had now come full circle, at the other end of the booth from where she had started.

Sean sighed, finished his lemonade, and stood up. There was no other choice but to intervene, or Ruth would move over one more time and be out of the booth altogether and end up on the floor. He leaned over the bar, grabbed a toothpick, put it into his mouth, and headed over to the redheaded American.

"WELL, Declan, it's not that I don't appreciate your offer," Ruth said, trying to muster some earnestness. "But I'm going to have to refuse."

"Now don't say no, Ruth. It makes perfect sense. You can stay with me while you're in Ireland. It will save you a bit of money and I'm perfectly happy to have you. I live alone, so the company would be nice and"—he raised his eyebrows— "it would be nice to have someone to cuddle with."

Ruth felt herself go pale as her stomach did a somersault. "Look, you are very nice, but as I've said all along, I'm not here to get involved with anyone," she said gently. "Besides, it wouldn't be fair to you as I'm leaving in six weeks."

Declan covered her hand with his and said, "We could certainly make the most of those six weeks."

Removing his hand, she said tightly, "Declan, I can't help but feel you're trying to take advantage of this situation."

Declan's smile disappeared. "Come on, don't be like that. We're both getting long in the tooth, and we don't want to put it off forever."

She might indeed be getting "long in the tooth" as he had said, but she wasn't easy and she certainly wasn't desperate. She was just about to tell him as much when she looked up, shocked to see Sean standing there.

"Ruth, are ye ready to go?" Hands in his pockets, Sean rocked back and forth on his feet. He never took his eyes off Declan.

Ruth found herself stunned, angry, and yet relieved. Angry that he had apparently followed her but relieved that she had an exit.

"Who is this?" demanded Declan.

"I'm Ruth's husband," Sean said with a grin.

Ruth closed her eyes in disbelief.

"Husband?" Declan answered, enraged. "In none of your letters did you ever mention a husband," he roared at Ruth.

Ruth glanced over at Declan, who resembled a bull with nostrils flaring. She could practically see steam spewing from his ears. All he needed to do to complete the picture was paw the floor with his foot.

"I think we're done here. Research! Ha!" Declan said. Standing up from the booth, he looked up at Sean, who towered over him. "Do you have children?"

Sean laughed, unable to help himself. "A bunch of them."

Ruth groaned.

Declan gave one final look at Ruth before departing. "You ought to be ashamed of yourself. You're a heartbreaker, missus." He stormed out of the bar.

Ruth looked up at Sean, who appeared to be enjoying himself.

Angrily, she grabbed her purse from the booth and headed to the bar to pay the tab. Sean was right behind her as she exited the premises.

"That was uncalled for!" she said over her shoulder, not stopping.

"It was obvious from where I was that you needed rescuing."

Ruth stopped abruptly and spun on him. "What exactly were you doing there? Following me? Spying on me?"

He didn't answer right away. His mouth started to open, but he thought better of it and shut it.

"And for your information, I do not need rescuing!" she said. "At least not by you!"

"I've done nothing but rescue you since you arrived on my doorstep!" he called after her.

She pushed through the doors of the hotel, wanting to put distance between her and Sean. How dare he invade her privacy? She grabbed the brass rail that ran along the steps. Her bad leg prevented her from bolting. Silently, she cursed it. Limping down the steps, she was sure she appeared weak and helpless, which she wasn't. It infuriated her. She didn't want any man to rescue her.

"You may have helped me, and I am grateful, but please do not say you rescued me," she said sharply as Sean caught up to her.

"Helped? Rescued? Aren't they the same thing?" he asked, clearly confused.

It was frustrating. She couldn't match his long-legged stride, and just trying to keep up with him caused her limp to become more pronounced. She gave up and slowed down, and was annoyed when he slowed down to keep in step with her.

"Is your leg bothering you?" he asked.

She ignored him. The last thing she wanted to do was talk about her leg.

He, too, remained silent as they walked to his car in the public carpark. She sank into the seat, glad to be off her feet. She closed her eyes, hoping to prevent Sean from talking to her. She didn't want to talk to him or to anyone at this point.

SEAN PULLED out of the carpark, stealing a glance at Ruth, who'd leaned her head against the window and closed her eyes. She hadn't spoken a word since they got in the car. He worked the toothpick in his mouth, trying to figure out what was going on in that head of hers. From time to time, he glanced over at her, enjoying the view. The creamy complexion, the dark lashes lying against it, and that fire-red hair.

He spoke first. "Look, I'm sorry for interrupting."

"If a person's eyes are closed it usually indicates they're sleeping," Ruth said.

"Or it's an avoidance tactic," Sean pointed out. "Anyway, he seemed a little overbearing."

Ruth couldn't argue with that. "Look, I really don't want to talk about it," she said.

"And he didn't really seem like your type," Sean continued.

Rolling her eyes, she said, "Again, it was just research." Sitting up straighter, Ruth looked over at him and said, "Besides, how do you even know what my type is?"

He laughed. "Clean-cut, business suits, maybe Ivy-league school. A gentleman."

"How did you figure that out?"

"Just a hunch," he said.

When she didn't say anything, he continued. "Sometimes it helps to talk about things. You know, get it off your chest? Clear the air?"

"The air doesn't need clearing, and my chest is fine."

He had to agree: it *was* fine. But he resisted stealing a glance at it. She wouldn't appreciate it after what she'd just been through with that gobshite.

"How about a cup of tea then?"

She opened her eyes and regarded him evenly. "Does a cup of tea solve all problems?"

He shrugged. "Usually."

"It would take more than a cup of tea to solve mine," Ruth said.

Sean laughed. She was funny, this American. "If it's more than a cup of tea you need, then I've got just the thing for you," he said. He was trying to cheer her up and he didn't know why he cared.

On the way out of Killarney, he whistled a tune to himself. Ruth was quiet on her side of the car. When they approached the next town over, he skipped the bypass and drove through town center, looking for a chipper. When he spotted one, he parked the car and got out without a word. Ten minutes later, he emerged with two portions of fish and chips wrapped in brown wrappers. Ruth watched him from the window with a frown on her face. He looked both ways and trotted across the street to the car.

Climbing in, he said, "Can you hold these for me, Ruth?"

"I'm not hungry," she said. As if on cue, her stomach gurgled.

"Your growling stomach says otherwise." He laughed.

He checked his rearview mirrors, looked behind him, pulled out of his spot, and headed out of town. Within minutes, as the road gradually rose, he pulled into a wide paved area off the main road, a lookout point. Nosing the car up to the low guardrail, he put it in park and turned off the ignition.

Neither said a word. Before them was spread an expansive green valley dotted with houses. The sky was a large swath of blue, and white clouds lazed in the sky. At the other end of the valley were dark, mysterious hills.

Ruth sat up taller in her seat. "Wow, that's really beautiful."

He took the bags of fish and chips and opened them in his lap. The tangy scent of vinegar filled the interior of the car. He handed her one of the greasy papers, then picked up his breaded cod wrapped in white paper and took a bite. Steam rose off of it.

"Now, tell your Uncle Sean what's bothering you."

She regarded him with horror.

"What?" he said, slightly offended. "I'm a good, impartial listener. It's a special set of skills I possess. Do you know the amount of people at the pub who have told me their problems? I'm like a priest in the confessional."

"Have you solved them all?" Ruth asked, unwrapping her food and eating a vinegar-soaked, salt-covered chip.

"No, of course not," he said. "Sometimes people just need for someone else to listen. Just to voice their problems, to hear them spoken out loud to another to share the burden, diffuses their power. It helps."

She didn't say anything for a while. But when she did, she gazed out the window at the scenery.

"I write romance for a living," she started.

He remained quiet. A trait of a good listener was to let the person tell their story in their own time.

"And yet, I have a hard time finding inspiration for my work," she said.

"Personally or professionally?" he asked.

"Both," she said immediately, then backtracked. "Well, mainly professionally. I was going through a dry spell back home, but then I found the ad for the marriage bureau and suddenly, I had loads of inspiration. I thought a change of scenery would be just what I needed."

"Until today," he said.

"Until today," she repeated. She took a bite of her fish. "This is delicious, by the way."

"Do you have more people to meet?" he asked, curious.

"A couple more," she said shyly.

Looking out the driver's-side window, he raised his eyebrows. She certainly was thorough.

"Chin up, there's hope," he said, taking a hearty bite of his fish.

She chewed thoughtfully. "I hope so."

"Look at it from a different angle," he suggested.

"How?" she looked at him. Against her pale skin, her deep green eyes were magnetic.

He shrugged. "The fella you just met? He probably wasn't what you envisioned as leading-man material?"

She shook her head.

"He obviously had an agenda," he said. "But what I'm saying is, you know what you don't want —I mean, in terms of a hero for your book."

"Right," she said.

"So, doesn't his example help you get a clearer picture of what you do want?"

They finished the rest of their fish and chips in silence, watching a dark bank of clouds roll in from the hills. The rain started.

"I guess we best head back," he said.

They wiped their hands on their napkins, then he took her wrappers from her, balled them up with his own, and threw them in the bag, tucking them behind his seat.

He tapped the pine-scented air freshener that hung from his rearview mirror. “Come on now, do your job.”

Ruth laughed. “You’re asking too much of it.”

He grinned. “All I can do is ask.”

# CHAPTER THIRTEEN

When they arrived back at the pub, Sean took one look at the darkened place and said, more to himself than to anyone, "Now that isn't right."

Ruth looked around. "What's that?" she asked.

He nodded toward the pub. Not even the outside lights were on. "Marie was to open up the pub today. I rang her yesterday. It's not like her to forget." He chewed on his toothpick.

"Have you checked your phone?" she asked.

Shaking his head, he pulled the car along the side of the building, throwing it into park and turning off the ignition. "Nah, I forgot it. It's on the bar."

Sean was worried. The pub really needed to be opened every night. Every bought drink added to his bottom line. Mondays were his only night off; he needed one night away from it all, where he could do what he wanted to do.

He was aware of Ruth behind him as he unlocked the front door of the pub. It was strange not to be alone. He had been alone for so long he had gotten used to it. But now with Ruth there, it was a feeling and a situation that he could not only get used to but enjoy as well. *Easy, lad,* he told himself. Those were dangerous thoughts, and no good could come from them.

The door sprung from the lock, and he felt around the inside wall for the panel of light switches and turned on the interior and exterior lighting. Ruth followed him inside, and he went behind the bar and grabbed his phone from where he'd left it, next to the cash register.

There were three missed calls from Marie. He dialed his voicemail and listened to his messages, frowning. Once that was done, he sighed and placed the phone on the counter.

"Is everything all right?" came Ruth's voice from the other side of the bar.

He shook his head. "No, it isn't. Marie's

daughter has gone into labor. The baby is about two months early, and they've been transferred to Temple Street in Dublin."

"Oh, that's awful," Ruth said.

"Yes, it is," he said. And it was. This was Marie's first grandchild, an event she'd been looking forward to since the tragic death of her husband years ago. It was all she could talk about, and rightly so.

He turned to Ruth, who regarded him curiously from her position on the bar stool.

"Did you want to go upstairs and watch some telly or something?" he asked. "It's quiz night tonight and it will be busy with locals. Although, it's the locals every night."

"No, thank you," she said. "If it's all right with you, I'd like to stay here in the pub. Do you mind?"

He regarded her for a moment: the red hair swept up in a messy bun, the creamy skin, and that ridiculous frock with all those flowers. He grinned. "Not at all." And that was the truth.

DESPITE THE FACT that Sean had been left short-handed, Ruth looked forward to an evening in the pub. The last thing she wanted to do was go upstairs and watch television while she was on vacation. And what better way to learn about the Irish people then to hang out in a pub that was frequented by locals?

She parked herself on a stool near the bar. Villagers slowly seeped in.

"What will you have to drink?" Sean asked, tapping his fingers on the bar.

"A Coke is fine," Ruth said.

From the corner of her eye, she watched him fix her drink. The long fingers grabbing a bar glass and putting some ice in it for her. "Ice in your drink—it's an American thing," he said, and gave her a wink and a grin. He took a slice of lime, gave it a slight squeeze, and laid it on top of her drink, sliding it across the bar to her. She imagined him giving her a light squeeze with those long, tapered fingers and she blushed.

There was no time for chat or banter, because customers soon lined the bar, and the booths began to fill up. It soon became apparent to Ruth that Sean had more customers than he could handle on his own. When he approached her to ask if she wanted another drink, she leaned forward across the bar and said, "Can I help you?"

He regarded her for a moment as if startled by her question.

She spoke rapidly, surprised to find that she was afraid of his rejection. "I've never worked in a bar before, but I have waited tables. Well, a long time ago."

He smiled at her and she melted. "Come on then, and I'll show you how to pull a pint."

Ruth slid off the stool, and Sean lifted the hinged portion of the counter for her so she could get behind the bar.

"Where's Marie?" someone asked.

"Grandbaby on the way, early," Sean answered.

"Aw, bless them," was the response.

Calvin's glass paused midair and he blanched. "Oh no." He stood up from his stool and pulled on his coat. "That baby means the world to her. I'll go and see if she needs me to do anything." And he was gone.

An elderly gentleman with the longest comb-over Ruth had ever seen took in the sight of her behind the bar. "It's about time you hired someone that's easy on the eyes," he said to Sean.

Sean pretended to be offended. "What are ye talking about? Aren't I easy on the eyes?" He batted his eyelashes.

"Yer nothin' but a big lump and a bollocks to boot," said another pub patron.

"What's your name?" asked another of Ruth.

"Ruth," she answered, delighting in the banter.

"American?" asked the other.

Sean nodded.

"You've gone exotic on us, Sean," said the man with the comb-over with a wink.

Both Sean and Ruth laughed.

Sean stood next to Ruth. "I'm going to give you a crash course in pulling a pint and operating the cash register."

Ruth nodded, excited to be rolling up her sleeves and helping out.

She tried to keep it all straight as Sean showed her where the liquor was, the measuring devices, how to use the soda gun. He pointed to where the lemons and limes were, where the clean bar glasses were, and where to put the dirty crockery. She just kept nodding, praying that she would remember it all.

She must have appeared alarmed, because he smiled at her and said softly, "It'll be grand, you'll see. Once the quizzing starts, it will quieten down a bit."

Taking a deep breath, she looked at him, unsure.

He smiled again and said, "It's just serving drinks, darlin'. You're not curing cancer here."

He clapped his hands. "All right, let's work on drawing down the perfect pint."

Ruth took a deep breath and told herself it was stupid to be intimidated by the simple act of pouring a beer. She didn't know why, but his opinion mattered to her. There was a sudden loud noise that sounded like the roof was going to come down, startling Ruth.

"It's just rain," Sean said, glancing up toward the ceiling. He then added with a grin, "It rains here a lot."

"I noticed," she said drily.

"Now grab your pint glass," he instructed.

Wildly, she looked around at the assortment of glasses underneath the bar. She stole a glance at the patrons seated at the bar and the type of glass they were using for their beer, stout, and ale. She grabbed the correct glass.

"Watch me," Sean commanded. "You hold the glass at a forty-five-degree angle and pull the tap forward. Let the draft hit the side of the glass, but don't let the tap touch the glass. Then when it's halfway full, straighten the glass out and fill it up. We don't want too much foam."

"Of course not," Ruth said.

"Now, your turn," he said. He stepped behind her and placed his arms around hers and his hands over her hands. He had stepped into her space. Her heartbeat picked up so rapidly that it thrummed in her ears, almost blocking the sound of his voice. His arms were long and strong, and Ruth swallowed hard, trying to concentrate on the task at hand. She could smell his scent, a heady combination of soap and shampoo and clean laundry.

"Now, let that foam settle down, take the money to the till, and then come back here, top it off, and hand it to the customer."

After a few tries, she managed to pour a perfect pint.

"Well done, Ruth," Sean said, clapping his hands.

There was an hour before the pub quiz started, but people continued to file in and take their places with their teams at their tables. The space behind the bar was narrow. Passing one another meant their bodies touched as they passed, usually with Sean's hands on Ruth's shoulders behind her.

The hour flew by, and Ruth pulled pints and poured drinks, sliding them across the bar. The rain continued to hammer on the roof, but it was drowned out by the loud chatter of the pub. At the start, she struggled with the cash register, but soon worked that out, as well. At busy times, when Sean sailed behind her with his own tasks to complete, he'd lay his hand on her shoulder, asking her how she was getting on. She'd smile and tell him truthfully that she was fine.

In all honesty, Ruth couldn't remember the last time she had had such fun. There was a lot of banter and camaraderie among the villagers, and Sean shone behind the bar.

After the quiz night ended and the crowd thinned out, Ruth sat down on one of the bar stools, next to the man in the corner, and thought how it felt good to get off her feet.

He wore a flat tweed cap on his head and a dark pullover sweater. He acknowledged her with a nod.

Sean handed her a glass of her own with a wink. Then he set another pint in front of the elderly man.

"Are you passing through?" the old man asked her.

Ruth smiled. "I'm not sure yet. I landed here quite by accident."

The old man regarded her and looked at his nephew. "There are no such things as accidents. If you landed here then the good Lord has a reason for it."

"I hope so."

"American?" he enquired.

She nodded.

"Do you have a husband or a boyfriend?" he asked, sipping from his pint glass.

She shook her head.

"You must be joking me," he said, unable to hide a look of disbelief. "A pretty girl like you? Not married?"

She shrugged and smiled. "I'm afraid not. Just haven't met 'the one.'"

"You will, mark my words."

They both sipped from their glasses and he asked, "Can I tell you about my Carmel?"

"Is Carmel your wife?"

He nodded. "She was. She's been dead for five years."

Ruth frowned. "Oh, I'm so sorry."

It was his turn to shrug. "It happens to all of us at some point. I know Carmel's waiting for me on the other side. Just passing the time until I meet up with her again."

Ruth squared her glass on the bar. "How did you meet her?"

He lifted his cap and scratched the top of his forehead. "Now that's a real interesting story. I met her at a dance at a crossroads. She was actually with another fella."

Ruth listened to his story and by the end of it,

both of them were laughing.

"And in the end, my bike had a flat tire and I had a black eye, but I got the girl, and that was the most important thing," he said with a grin, and he drained his glass.

Ruth couldn't help but agree with him.

AFTER THE AMERICAN girl left him, Mackie observed his nephew from the other side of the bar. Although Sean had been Carmel's nephew, he was just as much his. He was terribly fond of the lad. And because of that, he was also worried about him. It was time for his nephew to be settling down and starting his own family, not looking after his elderly uncle. Whenever Mackie had brought up the subject, Sean had joked about it. Said he had no intention of marrying. Ever. But it was no joke, thought Mackie. Of all people, he didn't want his nephew to end up alone. He sipped his beer. He was just hurting, that was all. Brid had done a terrible thing to him all those years ago, but the lad needed to put that in his past. It was time. Time to move on.

He whispered his silent prayer, more of an entreaty, the one he said every morning at Mass, that the good Lord would send his nephew the right woman. The kind of woman he himself had been married to: kind, and good to the core. He had been praying this prayer daily for years, since Brid had left Sean practically standing at the altar. He knew the Lord took His good time in answering prayers, but this was starting to border on the ridiculous.

He raised his pint glass heavenward. “Any time now.” His eye caught the form of the redheaded American. He sipped his beer, and thought she presented possibilities.

But he caught himself, looked up sharply, and said, “Don’t wind me up, Lord.”

BY MIDNIGHT, Sean had returned from driving his uncle home. Ruth had begun clearing tables, laying empty glasses on the bar. She wiped down each table and set the chairs right. She looked up to find Sean watching her with intensity, and she smiled warmly at him. While she cleared the tables, Sean swept the floors. After the last patron left, he turned off the outside lights and then bolted the doors shut.

As he turned toward Ruth, the lights went out, throwing the pub into pitch darkness. Ruth gasped, suddenly unsure of her surroundings or where she was in relation to them.

"Don't move," Sean said quietly. His deep voice in the darkness conjured up all sorts of intimate thoughts in Ruth and she blushed, grateful for the cover of darkness to conceal it. "This happens sometimes. We get too much rain and the power goes out. I'm sure it will be back on by morning."

She nodded, suddenly feeling foolish when she realized he couldn't see her nodding her head in the darkness.

Sean arrived at her side, taking hold of her hand. "I'll get you to your room," he said. "Follow me."

With her hand in his, she followed him around the bar, the path clear, through to the back hall and staircase, which were pitch black. He used his phone as a flashlight, creating a small path of illumination. He walked her to her bedroom door.

"Would you like a cup of tea?" he asked.

She shook her head. "No, thank you." She didn't want to point out that the electric kettle he had in his kitchen wouldn't work with the power out.

With her hand on the doorknob, she paused, not wanting the day to end. It had been a good one.

He lingered as well, seeming to be in no hurry to get to bed himself.

She looked up at him in the darkness. She could

make out the contours and shadows of his face. Even in the darkness, his eyes glittered.

"Good night, then," she said, opening the door and not wanting to be alone.

"Good night, Ruth," he said. "And thanks for all your help tonight. You're a sound mate."

She nodded again, slipping into the room and closing the door behind her. 'A sound mate?' He thought of her as one of the boys?

It wasn't long before she slipped under the bed-covers, noting the late hour, but she was wide awake. The sound of rain against a window was usually a sleeping potion for her, but tonight she felt as if she would never go to sleep. She stared at the window and the pattern the rain made on it, thinking about Sean.

There was a gentle knock on her door.

She sat up. "Yes?"

"May I come in?" Sean asked from the other side of the door.

"Yes."

The door opened, and Sean entered. He held up the hot water bottle in its fleece cover. "It'll be a damp night tonight, and you'll need this."

She frowned. "But where did you get the hot water from?"

He lifted up the blankets at the foot of her bed

and slid the jar in. “There’s a kettle on the range. The range is fueled by timber.”

“Oh.”

“Well, good night now,” he said, heading toward the door.

“Good night, Sean, and thank you,” she said.

He closed the door behind him, and Ruth lay awake for a very long time, thinking about him.

SEAN CLIMBED INTO HIS BED, exhausted, trying to push all thoughts of the redheaded American out of his mind. What had possessed him to call her “mate”? He cringed. A mate was one of the lads he played hurling, rugby, and soccer with through the local GAA. Ruth Davenport was a lot of things, but she was definitely not a “mate.” And when he had brought her a hot water bottle because he wanted her to be comfortable, she’d sat up, revealing a very feminine, flowery nightgown. With a laugh, he realized he’d never loved flowers more than in that moment when he saw them on her nightgown. More than anything, he’d wanted to climb in next to her in that big, comfy bed, and wrap his arms around her and pull her close.

The rain continued to pelt down outside, but it

did not distract him from his thoughts. No matter how hard he tried to think about something else, all his thoughts eventually drifted back to Ruth.

He sighed into the darkness, wide awake and restless. He clasped his hands behind his head, staring at the ceiling, unable to get the American girl out of his head.

# CHAPTER FOURTEEN

On Sunday morning, Ruth donned a white-and-lavender dress and paired it with a purple cardigan. She pulled on a pair of flats, then stood up and examined her tired face in the mirror.

Thoughts of Sean had kept her awake most of the night. She had climbed out of bed determined to park those thoughts in the dark recesses of her mind. She didn't care where they went, but she definitely wanted them removed from the prime, front-and-center real estate they were presently occupying.

She found him downstairs in the pub, but he wasn't doing publican-type things. He wore some kind of uniform, a long-sleeved polo shirt with the

Tipperary colors of blue and gold. But it was what was below the waist that caught Ruth's attention. He wore short white shorts that fit his legs like a glove, accentuating his powerful thighs. Ruth swallowed hard and forced herself to look away.

He looked up from where he was bent over with his foot on a bar stool, tying his shoelaces. He regarded her coolly.

"What's on the schedule for today?" she asked, smiling.

He put his foot down and stood up to his full height, showing off thick, powerful legs. Ruth tried not to stare. But it was just about impossible with him looking like the Colossus of Rhodes.

"I've got a match," he said.

"A match?" she repeated.

"A game. I play hurling every Sunday."

"Oh," she said. "What is hurling?"

"It's the Irish national sport."

Ruth would be the first to admit she had a hard time reading people. Observing people was one thing, but reading them was a set of skills all unto itself. But she would have bet money that he was acting indifferently toward her, so at odds with how he'd been before that she felt dismayed, and that bothered her. She decided the best course of action would be to ignore his changing temperament and take it all in stride.

"Could I go to this match of yours?" The village would be quiet on a Sunday, and the alternative was to hang around in the closed pub all day, waiting for him to return. She wasn't the waiting type.

He'd moved toward the exit and stood with his hand on the doorknob, looking as if he was going to bolt. He didn't say anything, and Ruth took a step closer to him.

"Maybe I could do something?" she said.

"Like what?"

She shrugged, raised her eyebrows, and smiled. "Oh, I don't know. Maybe I could keep score?" She leveled a gaze at him. "Or even hold your toothpick."

This elicited a grin from the publican. He opened the door and held it for her. "Come on, then, Ruth Davenport. Get your coat."

SEAN PULLED into the field in front of the local GAA's hurling pitch. The deluge of rain the past few days had soaked everything and left the field in a swampy, muddy state. Peering through the windshield, he saw men, women, and children of all ages, dressed in tracksuits, wellies, and raincoats. He looked over at the flame-haired foreigner occupying his passenger seat in her dress and flat shoes, and shook his head.

When he'd woken up that morning, he'd been determined not to let her get under his skin, not like she had been since she'd arrived. He had told himself to pull it together and not let himself be enchanted by this creature. But five minutes in her company and he had folded. What did that say about him?

Ruth watched all the villagers pouring onto the pitch. "I guess I'm not dressed appropriately."

"You'll need that raincoat." he said.

She nodded, lifting up the lightweight jacket from her lap.

It was too flimsy, Sean thought. More for show than purpose. "You're going to freeze," he said. "Do you not have anything heavier?"

She shook her head. "I'll be fine."

"It's too cold," he said.

"I'm wearing a cardigan," she pointed out. A quick glance told him there was no warmth in it.

Sean sighed. "I may have something in the boot of the car."

"The boot?" she repeated.

He thumbed behind him. "Back there."

"Oh, the trunk," she said knowingly.

"Yeah, the trunk."

They got out of the car and Sean circled around the back, popping open the trunk. He dug around inside and pulled out his wellies and a heavy, fleece-lined hoodie. Ruth had joined him and he could hear the mud sucking at her shoes. Looking down, he saw that they were now covered in muck.

"Do you not own boots or a pair of pants, woman?" he asked, slightly exasperated.

"I do, but I prefer dresses," she answered. "Besides, I packed my suitcase with clothing I thought would be suitable for the business I was carrying out."

He raised his eyebrows and she reddened. "I meant meeting and interviewing people."

He handed her the hoodie. "You better put this on."

Ruth pulled it on over her head and down over her dress and cardigan. It was way too big and she looked lost in it. He handed her his wellies. "Here, you'll have to wear these." He glanced at her feet and the size of his boots. "Wait a minute." She already had one shoe off and was leaning on the bumper of the car for support. Quickly, he grabbed a clean pair of socks from his gym bag, separated them, and stuffed one into the toe of each boot.

"This should do for now until we get you a proper pair of your own." He handed her a boot, and she slipped it on her bare foot. Then she slipped off the other shoe, handed it to him, and put on the other wellie.

She looked up at him and smiled. "Well, how do I look?" she asked. The hunter green wellies went up to her knees. "The green picks up the leaves on my dress."

He rolled his eyes. "Yeah, that's what I thought, too." He watched as she struggled to get her raincoat over his hoodie. It was too tight.

It started to rain and he handed her his own raincoat. "Here, take mine. It'll fit better."

She looked at him with uncertainty as she pulled on the raincoat. It went past her knees. "Won't the game be canceled because of rain?"

He shook his head. "If we canceled things because of the rain, nothing would get done in this country."

SEAN SLID THROUGH THE MUD, feeling the abrasion along his thigh, losing control of the ball and dropping his hurley stick along the way. The physicality of the sport was almost a relief and definitely a release, but most of all it was a distraction from his American guest. He got up and immediately cursed himself for looking for her in the crowd. He scanned the area where he had left her, in the front row of the stands. When his eyes finally landed on the flaming red hair, he was dismayed to see that she wasn't alone. That eejit, Frank Gleeson, stood at her side. Now what was he doing here? Not the sporty type, he had his hands in everything else, especially where women were concerned. Ruth laughed at something Frank said, and Frank leaned into her and whispered something in her ear, as if the two had known each other for years and were now sharing a secret joke.

"Come on, Hughes!" yelled one of his teammates.

Waking up, Sean leaned over and grabbed his hurley stick from the ground. Usually, he looked forward to playing sports every weekend. It was one of the ways he relaxed, but today he was in no humor for it.

Suddenly the match couldn't end fast enough for Sean.

~

"So that's hurling," Ruth commented as they made their way back to the pub. Sean sat in the driver's seat, his uniform caked with dried mud. He was unusually quiet, and she couldn't understand what she had done to make him angry.

He finally looked her way and said, "Did you enjoy it?"

She nodded and said a little too enthusiastically, "Oh I did." She dialed it down a bit and added, "Although I don't understand it, I did enjoy it." The truth was, she hadn't been able to take her eyes off of Sean. It was magnetic; he was in fine physical form. She enjoyed watching him but would never admit it, at least not to him.

She changed tack. "I met someone named Frank Gleeson. He said he's an auctioneer."

Sean's jaw tightened. "Be cautious around Frank; he's always looking for a way in," he warned.

"He seemed pleasant enough to me," she protested.

"Oh, he's pleasant enough all right, as you say."

"It was an innocuous enough conversation. We spoke about our mutual love of New York City."

"Mutual love, huh?" he asked. He pulled up to the pub and parked the car around the side.

Ruth stepped out of the car, still wearing Sean's

wellies, hoodie, and rain jacket. Oddly enough, she liked how it made her feel, wearing his jacket. It was intimate, like "going steady." Or something. The hoodie smelled most like him: of clean laundry and soap. It made her want to curl up and sleep in it.

Finally, she asked, "Do you want your jacket and boots?"

He gave her a quick glance and then headed toward the front door of the pub. His dismissive attitude wounded her. She didn't know what she had done wrong.

"Wait until you get inside, at least," he said. He pulled out his key ring and unlocked the front door. "When do you want to go to Dublin?"

She swept her hair back and decided that two could play at this game. "That's all right. If it's all the same to you, I'll just grab a bus up to Dublin. I thought I'd do some sightseeing while I'm there. I don't want to impose on your hospitality any further," she said evenly.

He shook his head. "It's not an imposition. We made a bargain, and I will drive you to Dublin tomorrow as promised."

"We'll see," she said, removing his coat, hoodie, and boots and heading up the stairs to her room.

~

Ruth spent the rest of Sunday staying out of Sean's way. She hunkered down in the corner of the pub, laptop open, working on her book. The writing was flowing, and she smiled to herself. Her hero and heroine were coming naturally to her. But after a writing sprint, she reread what she had written and sat back with a gasp, horrified to find that her male character strongly resembled Sean Hughes.

"Everything all right?" Sean asked, standing at her table.

Surprised at the interruption, she snapped the laptop closed and looked up at him. "Everything's fine. Just a character who is going off script."

"We can't have that, can we?" he asked. "Look, you've been over here for a couple of hours. Do you want something to eat or drink?"

She shook her head.

He regarded her for a moment before turning to go.

"Sean?"

He turned back.

Elbow on the table, she scratched her forehead. "You know, I think I can take the bus tomorrow. No need to waste your day off."

"I'm not wasting my day off," he said. "I

promised to drive you around, and I always keep my promises."

*Oh.*

~

THE FOLLOWING MORNING, Ruth relented and allowed Sean to drive her to Dublin to meet Majella, a member of the marriage bureau. From the start, Majella had been open to helping Ruth with her research. Her letters had been chatty and upbeat and Ruth found herself looking forward to meeting the Irish woman. As a thank-you, Ruth had gathered a bag of her paperbacks to gift to her.

In a good mood, she chose a dress the Irish color of emerald green, liking the way it suited her hair color, and topped it off with a matching cardigan.

When she arrived downstairs, Sean said, "I've got to make one quick stop before we head to Dublin."

"That's no problem," she said, following him out to the car.

They drove down a winding, isolated dirt passageway, and Sean parked the car in front of a yellow farmhouse. Ruth stepped out of the car to get a closer look at the colorful rose garden out front, and breathed deeply as the fragrance greeted her.

Wordlessly, she followed Sean toward the back of the house, down a loose gravel path bordered by a hawthorn hedge. About fifty feet along the path, Sean ducked under an opening in the hedge. Ruth did the same, and stepped out onto the other side to find row after row of fruit trees. Sycamores and hawthorns created a natural fence around the orchard. Ruth looked around. The trees were young, with no fruit on them, and there had to be hundreds of them.

"This is amazing," Ruth said. She fingered a leaf on one of the trees.

Sean stood among them and smiled proudly. "These are my apple trees."

"What are they for?"

"The plan is to become a grower," he said. "I lease the land from Mackie."

"Is it all the same type of apple?"

He shook his head. "Those are Tipperary Pippin over there. And that's Elstar in the last row, and the rest are Dabinett, apples grown specifically to make cider."

Ruth had never seen him so animated. She took a good look around at Sean Hughes's passion. And the unexpected thing was that the publican looked so at home in the orchard. He bent down and inspected the base of one of the trees.

"Have they borne fruit yet?" she asked.

"Not yet," he answered, standing up and brushing his hands off on his pants. He looked around the place with what Ruth would describe as a look of adoration. "I've only planted them last year. I'm hoping to see some fruit in a couple of years."

She closed her eyes and imagined the sight of all those trees, lush and fragrant with apples. Opening her eyes, she realized she wouldn't be here to see the fruit, and that disappointed her.

He came over and stood next to her, looking down the row of trees.

"Is it a lot of work?" she asked.

"It's not work if you love it," he replied.

She knew what he meant. She felt the same way about writing.

He continued talking. "I come by every morning to check on things."

"You do?"

He nodded and smiled at her. "I'm back before you wake up."

"Did you have to take any courses?" she asked, suddenly curious.

"I did," he said, taking in the sight of his apple

trees laid out neatly before him. "Took some horticulture classes and did a six-month internship with a grower up north."

"Who managed the pub?"

"Well, I was able to cobble something together between Marie and my brothers."

He turned and headed out of the orchard, and Ruth had no choice but to follow him.

When they reached the car, she nodded toward the house.

"Did you want to stop in and say hello to your uncle while you're here?" she asked.

Sean looked over at the house and shook his head. "Nah." He jumped into the car and Ruth did the same.

"It would only take a minute, Sean," she protested. "It doesn't seem right to be here and not say hello."

He looked at her and grinned. "You're absolutely right. Where are my manners?"

She went to get back out of the car but he reached over and laid his hand on her arm. His touch was warm, and she resisted the urge to put her hand over his.

"I'm teasing you, Ruth. He's not home. He went down to Kerry for the day with the retirement group," Sean explained.

"Why didn't you tell me?" she asked.

"Because you didn't give me a chance to," he said with a laugh.

He was still laughing when they drove out of the passage.

# CHAPTER FIFTEEN

Sean couldn't shake the image of the American standing in the middle of his orchard. Two beautiful things together. She'd looked like she belonged there, and that scared him.

He realized he had played it too cool with her when she said she'd take the bus to Dublin. *No way*, he'd thought. There was no way she was going off to meet strange men by herself. He tried not to examine his motivations too closely, telling himself that he was just concerned about his guest's safety.

He glanced over at her in the passenger seat, but she stared straight ahead. He chuckled to himself.

Her head turned sharply to him. "What is so funny? Why are you always laughing at me?" Even in the bright afternoon light, he could see her eyes were ablaze. She was something else, that was for sure.

He shook his head, working the toothpick in his mouth. “I’m not laughing at you, Ruth Davenport.”

“And would you stop calling me that?” she pleaded. “You can just call me Ruth.”

“Kind of touchy today, aren’t you?” he asked.

“I am not touchy,” she said firmly.

He couldn’t help himself. “Maybe you’ve a case of the nerves about meeting this fella.”

She went quiet on him again, and he stared at her for a minute. Never had he seen anyone who could do so much for a color as she did for the color green. She looked dynamite. That red hair! She had pinned the sides of it to the back of her head and let it fall just below her shoulders. He’d be hard pressed to find another woman as beautiful as she. At times, she took his breath away.

THE DRIVE to Dublin took a little more than two hours. They arrived by mid-afternoon, but the traffic was horrific in the city center. Sean navigated it with ease, managing to drop only a few expletives along the way. Ruth raised her eyebrows several times in response but said nothing.

Majella had agreed to meet her at a park just inside the capital. Ruth had suggested the venue. The weather forecast had called for unseasonably warm sunshine and no wind, and Ruth had decided she wanted to be outside. She felt the need for some fresh air.

When they arrived, he found a spot outside the park. He pulled the newspaper out of the backseat. "I'll be right here. Just come out when you're ready."

Ruth reminded herself not to be nervous. After all, Majella had seemed so kind in her letters.

Ruth climbed out of the car, a little unsteady.

She leaned back inside and asked, "You're not going to follow me into the park? Show up unannounced?"

Sean shook his head. "I promise, I'll remain right here."

She was about to close the door when he leaned across the middle console and said in an affected American accent, "Go get 'em, Tiger!"

Ruth narrowed her eyes. "That is not helpful."

"Right then." He nodded, unfurling his newspaper. "Carry on!"

"Ugh," she intoned, exasperated. As she

slammed the car door, she could hear him laughing. Still shaking her head, she made her way to the entrance gates of the park.

The sight before her calmed her. It was a beautiful, golden autumn day. Despite it being October, there was some warmth to the sun and the grass was still a lush green. A diverse group of people was taking advantage of the weather: mothers and fathers pushed young children in strollers, college students gathered on park benches or sprawled on blankets on the grass, and pensioners grouped around the tables to play cards or have a chat. There was the soundtrack of children's laughter, interspersed with the buzz of snippets of conversation.

Majella had told her to meet her by the water fountain. She spotted it in the distance, wishing it wasn't so far away. As she got closer, she scanned the area looking for someone who resembled the photo. On the other side of the fountain, she caught sight of a woman with her purse slung over her shoulder and her arms crossed in front of her chest. There was a pair of sunglasses perched on top of her blonde head.

When she reached her, her direction had shifted and she needed to shield her eyes against the afternoon sun. "Majella?"

The woman nodded and said with a smile, "You

must be Ruth." Majella was a pretty woman who was taller than Ruth and older, maybe in her late forties or early fifties.

"Would you like to sit down?" Ruth asked tentatively, studying her.

"Yes, that would be lovely," she said.

They sat down on a wrought iron park bench.

"I don't understand what your problem is," Majella said, looking at her.

Confused, Ruth looked at her. "Excuse me?"

"Why you need help in landing a man?" Majella said. She added quickly, "You're a very pretty girl. I'd think they'd be flocking to you."

Before Ruth could protest, the other woman laid her hand on Ruth's arm. "I'd be happy to give you some tips, Ruth."

"Tips?" Ruth repeated, trying not to burst out laughing.

Majella nodded. She looked pointedly at Ruth, her eyes widening and eyebrows lifting with an expression that read, "you know."

Ruth felt it was best to go back to the beginning. "You do know that I write romance and am doing research?"

Majella regarded her. "So, you are actually a writer? Of romance?" She shook her head and laughed. "I thought it was a cover story."

Ruth smiled and handed her the bag of books. “Nope. It’s all on the up and up.”

Majella looked in the bag and glanced quickly at Ruth. “I am so sorry.” Then she burst out laughing. “It’s funny, me offering to give you advice when I’m looking for love myself.” She paused and said, “Anyway, thanks for the books.”

“Have you had any luck with the marriage bureau?” Ruth asked.

“Not yet,” Majella answered. “But I’m hopeful.”

The woman was attractive and chatty and Ruth had a hard time believing she wasn’t in a relationship.

“What led you to the marriage bureau?”

Majella looked away and for a brief second, sadness flitted across her face. “I wasn’t having any luck in my own social circle. It’s the same people all the time. I thought it would be a good way to expand my circle and meet other people.”

“How long have you been with the bureau?”

“Almost six months. I’ve met a few men but so far, no sparks,” she replied. “And that’s very important.”

Ruth nodded.

Looking around, Majella said. “I’m looking for the whole package. Chemistry and companionship.”

Looking thoughtful, she added, "I love my life. I have a nice career, a nice family, and a nice home. But I want to share all that with someone."

Her thoughts drifted to Sean, sitting outside the park in his car, waiting for her, as she considered what Majella said in regards to chemistry and companionship.

SEAN WAS JUST TURNING the page of the A section of the *Irish Independent* when he caught sight of Ruth exiting the park with a blonde-haired woman at her side. He regarded them curiously. Both women chatted away as if they'd been lifelong friends. Funny, but he'd thought it was only men Ruth was meeting for her research. The feeling of relief that washed over him at the sight of Ruth with a woman instead of a man concerned him. He hadn't cared for a woman since Brid. And he'd vowed not to care for one again. But the redhead had turned things upside down for him.

He folded up the paper and threw it into the backseat.

When they approached the car, Ruth opened the door and introduced Majella to Sean.

The other woman looked at Sean and then back to Ruth and broke into a grin. “Why Ruth, you’ve got yourself a big, strapping lad.” She winked at Ruth, who blushed.

Sean watched in amusement as Ruth stammered out an explanation. “Sean is helping me.”

Majella looked back and forth between the two of them and shrugged. “If you say so.”

The women said their goodbyes and promised to keep in touch.

Ruth climbed into the car and without a word, she pulled the seat-belt strap forward and buckled herself in.

“How did it go?” Sean asked, leaning back against the door, toothpick hanging from his mouth.

“It went well. She was helpful,” she said.

Sean looked over at her, admiring the view. Her style of dress was quirky, he had to admit, but also definitely very feminine. He had yet to see her in a pair of pants, but he was fine with the frocks. She had a great pair of legs.

“I thought you were meeting a man,” Sean said.

“I thought it was important to interview both men and women about why they would resort to a marriage bureau to get their HEA,” Ruth explained.

“HEA?” he repeated, not comprehending.

"All romance books have a 'happily ever after,'" Ruth explained. "It's part of the formula. If it doesn't have a happy ending, it isn't romance. More like women's fiction."

"Would you like an HEA?" he asked.

"Of course."

"I'm sure you'll get it," he said.

She turned to him and narrowed her eyes. "Do you even believe in happily ever after?"

"No," he said truthfully. He wasn't going to lie to her. She didn't deserve that. He added quickly, "Not for me at least."

"But why shouldn't you be happy?"

He grinned. "Who says I'm not happy?"

"I mean happy in love," she explained.

"Oh that," he said. He started up the car. The last thing he wanted to do was have a conversation about his love life.

"You're foregoing any future romance based on one bad experience," she pointed out.

"Getting dumped three weeks before your wedding is pretty bad," he said.

"Well, I'd say the problem is hers and not yours," she said.

"She probably didn't know a big, strapping lad when she saw one."

Ruth laughed and clapped her hands. He wished

she would do more of that. She was absolutely luminescent when she laughed.

"Can we get on the road now?" he asked.

Sean took a different route back toward Tipperary. He wanted her to see some of the beautiful countryside, because to him there was no better scenery to be found. It would add half an hour to their trip, but he didn't mind.

After a while, she looked out the window and said with a sigh, "I have never seen a prettier place. The scenery is amazing. I never get tired of looking at it."

He grinned, observing her, and thought the same thing about her. "This is called the Golden Vale."

"It's easy to see why. It's breathtaking."

He was chuffed that she should think so. For whatever reason, her opinion of his country mattered to him.

"What's that up there?" she asked, indicating a set of ruins on an elevated site. She sat forward in her seat.

"That's the Rock of Cashel," he said. "Home to the Munster kings. There are centuries-old buildings there, including a chapel and the ruins of a cathedral."

"It looks amazing," she said, not taking her eyes

off of it.

Inspired, Sean asked, "Would you like to see it?"

She turned to him. "Really? You don't mind? I mean, I could get a taxi or a bus here another day."

He shook his head. "Not at all. Come on. It's a sight worth seeing."

He headed into the town of Cashel and then followed the signs to the site. It had been a few years since he'd been there, and he was only too happy to show it to her. He made his way to the carpark at the base of the hill on which sat the magnificent ruins. There was a climb up a slight ascent, and he wondered about her leg. Not for the first time, he wondered about her footwear. He shook his head. How did she get along at home in the winter, with the snow? The woman probably didn't even own a proper pair of boots.

The carpark wasn't even half full. There weren't a lot of tourists around in October. They got out of the car and he locked it, then went to the back, pulled out his rain jacket, and handed it to her.

"That's not necessary," she protested.

"Yes, it is," he said, still holding it out to her. "It will be cold up there at the top of the hill. And windy."

"No, seriously, I'll be fine," she said. "I've got my sweater."

He shrugged and pulled the jacket on himself. In case she changed her mind, and he suspected she would, he'd bring it along. It would just be easier to wear it.

As they climbed the slight incline to the cathedral ruins at the top, a bracing wind swept up alongside them. Sean's eyes watered with the rush of the wind. Ruth pulled her cardigan tighter around her, and her dress whipped around her.

"Boy, that's some wind," she said.

"It is," he said. He lacked the heart to tell her it would be much worse at the top. The wind was something to contend with, but hopefully, she'd soon forget about that when she saw what was at the top.

A massive stone wall circled the site. They climbed up a small wooden staircase and found themselves inside a reception area. A tour guide stood behind the counter.

Sean proceeded to take his wallet out of his pocket, but Ruth laid her hand on his arm.

"Please, let me pay for this. You've driven me all over and provided me with bed and board," she said. "Please, let this be on me."

"All right then, I won't argue with you," he said amiably.

"Thank you," she said.

They stood with a couple of German tourists and waited patiently for the guide to start. First, they stepped out into the main courtyard, which featured a replica of an ancient stone cross, now weather-beaten. In front of them stood the roofless remains of a thirteenth-century cathedral and the twelfth-century Cormac's Chapel, the oldest surviving chapel in the country. After a brief stop in a damp, low-ceilinged room with tiny windows for a short audio-visual presentation from the Office of Public Works, the tour guide led them to Cormac's Chapel. Ruth craned her neck to study the still-intact ceiling and the fragments of long-ago murals that had survived centuries of Irish weather and British occupation. Sean had been there many times before, but the place never failed to impress him. All that history and passage of time.

Ruth looked at him, smiling, and something within him melted. "I'm trying to imagine what it was like here eight hundred years ago," she said.

He smiled. The American had practically read his mind.

"I mean, for something like this to stand here

for so long. It's like a silent witness to all that history," she enthused. "It's staggering."

"That it is," he agreed.

He didn't know what mesmerized him more: his surroundings or her reaction to it. It was wonderful to watch her discover it for the first time.

They followed the tour guide from the chapel to the cathedral ruins. The walls and the arched Gothic windows were still intact, but the glass panes were long gone. The tour guide gave them a brief rundown of the history of it, and then left them to their own devices. He instructed them to meet him in the small anteroom next to the reception area. Ruth walked around, looking up at the walls and running her hands along the stone. The wind whistled outside.

After fifteen minutes, they headed outside from the cathedral. There were tombstones littering one corner of the site, some of them recent. Ruth stepped away from the shelter of the buildings, taking in the view of the lush green valley below. A sigh escaped her lips.

"It's so beautiful that words are inadequate," she said. He stood behind her and she stepped away, pointing to the pile of stone ruins below in the valley. "What is that?"

"That's Hore Abbey," he replied.

As she stepped closer to the stone wall, a gust of wind blew in and lifted up the skirt of her dress so that it was practically around her shoulders. Ruth's hands came down quickly, forcing the bottom part of her dress back into place, but not before Sean got a brief eyeful of a great set of legs, one of which had several scars running the length of it, and a pair of lacy white knickers that hugged Ruth's bottom. He glanced heavenward and said with a grin, "Thank you, Lord, for that."

When she turned around, he saw that her face was beet red. Without a word, he took off his coat and handed it to her.

She grumbled a "thank you," pulled it on, and marched off in the direction of the buildings. Sean walked behind her, shaking his head and smiling.

RUTH WAS MORTIFIED. The wind had conspired against her. She picked up her pace and sought shelter inside, away from the punishing gusts. Her hair was all out of place. She felt around for her barrette at the back of her head, unclipped it, and smoothed her hair back into place as best she could without the benefit of a mirror, reclipping the barrette into place. She caught Sean watching her and frowned at him.

She stepped into the small antechamber, a brightly lit room with a low ceiling and white walls. She moved along the displays from artefact to artefact, marveling at the age and good condition of some of the items. When the tour guide began to talk, Ruth took a spot against the wall, leaning for a moment next to a dark gray slab of what appeared to be an obese, naked female form.

The day had taken its toll, and Ruth was beginning to wilt. What she wouldn't give for a hot cup of tea and a nice hot bath. And a hot water bottle at the foot of her bed to rest her weary feet on. Her legs were cold, and she had no one to blame but herself. She hadn't dressed for sightseeing in this unpredictable, changeable Irish weather.

The tour guide was explaining some of the various items and artefacts kept there. He nodded to Ruth with a grin. "That statue you're standing next to? The one you touched earlier?"

Ruth's back stiffened at the thought of being called out in front of everyone and the possibility of being chastised.

But the tour guide, an older man, possibly retired, kept smiling. "That's what we call a *Sheela na gig*; it's a Celtic fertility goddess. And the rumor is, anyone who stands near it or touches it will be pregnant within a year." He winked at Ruth.

Ruth stepped away from it as if burned, and looked at Sean, who burst out laughing.

"I think I'm ready to go home," she said, and she made her way to the exit with Sean behind her, still laughing.

# CHAPTER SIXTEEN

Sean had told Ruth he had a few things to do and would be gone for a while. He'd also written the McGonagle farm address on a piece of paper and handed it to her, asking her to call the hire company about collecting the car.

He had two stops to make. First, he was going back to the McGonagle farm to sort out Ruth's car. Second, he was driving over to Clonmel to meet with a representative of Bulmers cider makers to gather information.

He was determined to get Ruth's car. He didn't care if he ran into Brid or not. Restless energy flowed through him. He felt unsettled.

Sean approached the front door of the McGonagle farm. He took his toothpick out of his mouth before he knocked.

"Who is it?" demanded Mr. McGonagle.

"Sean Hughes."

"Go away!"

"Open the door," Sean instructed. "I want to talk to you."

The old man was slow to comply. He peered out at Sean. "You again. Brid isn't here."

"I've not come for Brid."

"Not yet, anyway," the old man said.

"I've come about the car."

The old man began to shut the door, but Sean was quicker in stopping it with his foot.

"I'm just here to inform you that I'm arranging for the hire company to send a truck out to collect the car."

"I'll not allow them on my property."

Sean looked away, sighing. He reminded himself that the man before him was old and infirm. Finally, he turned back and said, "You will. The car will be collected this week."

"Says who?" Mr. McGonagle demanded.

"Says me," Sean replied through gritted teeth. "If there are any problems removing the car, I'll come back with the guards and tell them you are in possession of stolen property."

The old man's face turned red. "You wouldn't dare."

"I would." Sean took his foot from the door and, satisfied, he left, with the old man staring after him.

~

THE PUB WAS QUIET. Sean kept his eye on Ruth in the corner, looking intently at her laptop. Her fingers flew over the keyboard. He stood at the bar, talking to his uncle about his meeting with the cider representative. It had been encouraging and that had put Sean in a good mood. The meeting had lasted an hour and the rep had given him a tour as well as his business card, telling him to contact him anytime. The irony of the Bulmers company being located in Clonmel as well as the marriage bureau was not lost on Sean.

Ruth approached the bar and asked for a bottle of water. She soon returned to her seat, her dress swaying gently with her stride.

"It's a shame about her bum leg," Mackie said from his corner.

Sean looked away from Ruth. "It's only a shame if you want her for racing."

Mackie laughed. "I'm familiar with that look on

your face. I had it once too, a long time ago at a dance at the crossroads."

"Now, Mackie, I think that's the drink talking."

His uncle laughed. "Maybe." He paused, eyed Sean and said, "And then, maybe not."

~

SEAN SAT in the chair next to the range with his long legs up on the table. He heard Ruth coming down the hall, so he sat up and put his feet down. From her position in the doorway, she looked around the room as if deciding whether she should enter or not. Indicating the chair on the other side of the range, Sean said, "Have a seat. The kettle is hot."

Ruth put her hands on her hips. "You drink a lot of tea."

He smiled. "I like it. Plus, it's a pleasurable way to pass the time."

Slowly, she made her way over to the chair and sat down. As she crossed her legs, he noticed her wince. The dresses she wore did not cover the scars on her leg. They had faded, leaving thick, white marks. But to Sean, they looked fine. It was a part of who she was.

"Can I ask you a personal question?" he asked.

She gave him a small smile but seemed hesitant, as if he was going to ask her something too personal. She folded her hands in her lap and tilted her head and regarded him. "What did you want to ask me, Mr. Hughes?"

He nodded toward her leg and watched as she shifted it behind her good leg. He found the action oddly intimate, and nearly lost the power of speech. "What happened to your leg?"

She looked down at it as if she were seeing it for the first time. "When I was sixteen, I was in a car accident. I was out with friends, and my friend went through a stop sign. We were hit by a truck, and my leg was broken in many places. It was put back together with lots of pins and rods, which is why it's kind of stiff. Unfortunately, an infection developed in the wound, so the recovery took a long time."

"It sounds horrific," he said.

She drew in a deep breath. "It was. Between the hospital and then rehab, I was out of commission for over a year. When you're sixteen, it's not an ideal situation."

"What about the other people in the car?"

"They were fine. We were lucky no one was killed. It put everything in proper perspective."

"And your leg?" he asked gently. She was skittish, like a newborn colt. There was something about this topic that made her nervous. He wondered what he could do to put her at ease.

"This is as good as it's going to get." She laughed nervously. "So, no dancing for me."

"It's overrated anyway," he said, trying to make light of it. "I've got two left feet myself."

She laughed and he was relieved.

"But it wasn't all bad. The year I spent recovering I also spent reading. I read tons of books. There wasn't much else to do."

"Did you start writing then as well?" he asked.

"I did."

Deciding that tea was called for, he stood up and poured some hot water from the kettle into the teapot, and pulled down two mugs from the French dresser. By now he knew how she took it, and he fixed it accordingly. He also knew that she liked a sweet with her tea, and although he had no cake or tart, there was always a box of Jaffas on hand for when his nieces and nephews visited. He plated two up and handed them to her.

She looked up to him, her green eyes blazing under the dark lashes, and he'd have liked nothing better than to cup her face and lay a kiss on those sweet lips.

She took the teacup and plate from him, and he turned around, slightly embarrassed, and cleared his throat as if there were something stuck there. The truth was, there was something stuck there: all the things he wished he had the courage to say to her. With teacup in hand, he settled back into his seat.

"Does your leg hurt?" he asked.

She bit into one of the cookies and frowned, looking at it and then at him. "Is that orange marmalade?"

He nodded. "It's really the national biscuit," he said, referring to the biscuit base with a thin layer of marmalade, covered in dark chocolate.

"It's yummy," she said.

He laughed. She said that about everything sweet.

"Anyway, my leg doesn't hurt that much. It's mostly stress that makes it ache."

He tucked that away for future reference. He sipped his tea and waited for her to continue. He didn't want her to think he was prying. But he was curious. He wanted to know everything about her. The night she landed on his doorstep in the middle of the rainstorm played over and over again in his mind. He couldn't help but think how his life had been turned upside down since her arrival. Reluctantly, he conceded to himself that he'd needed some shaking up.

"I think it holds me back," she admitted, finishing the last Jaffa.

"Why do you say that?" he asked.

She shrugged and looked nervously around. "Not anything I can put my finger on specifically. It's just that there are some things I can't do."

"Like what?"

"Well, I can't run." She laughed that sweet laugh of hers. "Well, I could, but it would involve me dragging my leg behind me."

It was his turn to shrug. "Were you a runner before the accident?"

She burst out laughing. "Not on your life! I was more of a reader than an athlete. Actually, the word 'athlete' and my name shouldn't be spoken in the same sentence." She giggled, and he was pleased to see her loosen up a bit about her leg. He couldn't help but laugh along with her.

"And stairs can be tricky, especially if there's a lot of them," she said.

Lifting his teacup, Sean pronounced, "Then let's be glad there's only one flight of stairs here as opposed to two."

She lifted her own cup and clinked it against his.

~

RUTH HAD an appointment to meet Paul Reilly, an accountant by trade and a member of the marriage bureau. His letters were short and basic, more a trading of information than anything, so unlike the chatty letters of Majella. He had asked her to meet him on his lunch hour in Cork City.

She gave Sean the name of the restaurant and the shopping plaza where it was located.

Sean nodded. "I know it well. They have a big garden center there. While you're meeting your fella, I can take a stroll around the nursery."

"Perfect," Ruth replied.

She and Sean chatted amiably on the drive down. Ruth was glad she no longer had the rental car. She was grateful to be driven around, as it gave her a chance to enjoy the scenery. She never tired of looking at it.

When they pulled into the shopping center, Sean said to Ruth, "I'm going into the garden center, but I'll leave the car unlocked in case you should get back before I do."

"Okay, thanks," she said. She pulled down the visor and took a quick look in the mirror.

"You look fine," Sean said.

Ruth blushed and glanced at him. "Thank you."

They parted ways, and Ruth watched as Sean strolled away in the opposite direction, hands in the pockets of his jacket. She turned and headed toward the café to meet Paul Reilly.

"Ruth?" someone called out as she approached the door.

She turned toward the voice, smiling.

Wow.

Paul Reilly closed the distance between them. He was handsome in a way that hadn't been apparent in his photo, with his auburn hair and his amber eyes. Exotic. Ruth approved of the rest of his look, as well: clean-cut and business casual.

He extended his hand. "You must be Ruth Davenport."

Shaking his hand, she said, "And you must be Paul."

He smiled, revealing straight white teeth. "Guilty. Shall we get something to eat?"

Ruth nodded. He held the door for her and once they were inside, they were promptly seated.

"I have to admit to being really nervous about meeting you," Paul said.

"Me? Really? Why?" she said in disbelief.

"Lots of reasons," he said. "But especially with you being a successful writer. I can only dream of doing what you do for a living."

Ruth blushed and looked down at the table. "Thank you."

Over lunch, they discussed her research at length. He was a gem, she thought, as he was so transparent about his desire to find his soulmate and settle down. He answered her questions politely. After their desserts were laid down in front of them, he leaned forward and rubbed the back of his neck. With both a frown and a funny smile, he said, "Actually, Ruth, I have a confession to make."

"Oh?" she said, mentally bracing herself.

He nodded. "I really wanted to meet you because I was hoping to pick your brain about writing."

Relief flooded through Ruth and she relaxed. "No problem. Do you want to be a writer? A published writer?"

"Yes, more than anything," he said.

"I thought you were an accountant," she said.

"It pays the bills," he said with a grimace.

Ruth felt compassion for him. She took a bite of her pear-and-almond tart. "Have you written anything?"

He nodded. "I'm enrolled at university, taking a creative writing course." He sipped his tea. "I have started writing a book."

"Well done, that's a start," she encouraged.

Ruth remembered how it was for her before she had gotten her book deal with a publisher. It had been difficult when she'd first started out. Writing was a lonely business and by sheer luck, she'd landed an agent, and then a publisher. The support came after, but she could have used it before. She wanted to help him in the same way she had wanted someone to help her back at the start of her own career.

"I've always been an avid reader, since primary school," he said.

That was usually how it started: with a love of reading.

"What genre do you write in?" she asked.

"I write thrillers," he said, his face becoming more animated.

"Good," she said. "Look, Paul, I'd be happy to help you in any way I can."

"That's generous of you, Ruth," he said, smiling.

"Would you like me to take a look at what you've written?" she asked.

"Yes, that'd be great," he said.

They finished their desserts and tea and headed out of the restaurant, agreeing to meet up again so Paul could hand off his work to her to critique.

~

SEAN HAD LOST track of time in the garden center, strolling through the aisles, pricing plum trees, and comparing permanent and temporary tree stakes. When he glanced at his phone, he figured he'd better get a move on. He didn't want to keep Ruth waiting too long.

He planned to take her to Killaloe, on the Clare-Tipperary border, one of the most beautiful spots in the country. He wanted to show her the sights, including the Lakeside Hotel, which did a nice lunch and dinner.

Whistling as he walked to the car, he frowned when he noticed she wasn't in it. Quickly, he looked around, but didn't spot her anywhere. He pulled out his phone. Her hour wasn't up yet. Maybe her meeting was going okay.

He sat in the car, waiting. The sky was overcast and the air was heavy with damp. Another fifteen minutes passed before she emerged from the restaurant with a tall man. The guy looked familiar. Sean studied him and then it dawned on him. He resembled the kind of men who appeared on the covers of Ruth's books. The two of them were chatting, and Sean was not too far away to notice the way the guy leaned into her. The way he smiled at her with a look of pure admiration. Ruth, for her part, was smiling and seemed relaxed.

Then the man leaned in and gave her a kiss on the cheek, and Ruth did not object. It was a chaste kiss, one even the nuns would approve of. *If that were me, I'd kiss her properly,* Sean thought, annoyed. *By the time I was finished, she'd have no doubt about me, her, or us.*

Sean chewed on his toothpick. This was not good.

As Ruth walked back toward the car, he noticed she looked much softer.

*Damn.*

Once she got into the car, he asked as nonchalantly as possible, "Did it go well?"

She nodded, smiling. "It did. He's very nice. We'll probably go for dinner at the end of the week."

"Nice."

"Where to now?" Ruth asked.

He looked at her and forced a smile. "Might as well head back to the pub."

He was quiet all the way home, thinking of all the things he wanted to say to her.

THE PUB on a weekday afternoon was quiet enough, with only a handful of locals. Sean was busy going back and forth to the back room, and had asked Ruth to mind the bar. He had gone quiet on her the last few days, and she wasn't sure what was on his mind.

A couple of the regulars pulled stools together in the middle of the pub floor. Two men left the pub and returned with musical instruments.

Sean appeared, hands on his hips. "Is it a session then?"

When they nodded, he leaned across the bar and said to Ruth, "Darlin', would ye hand me those two spoons to the right of the cash register?"

She scanned the area next to the register, and sure enough, there were two tablespoons tucked off to the side.

She held them up. "These?" she asked, eyebrows raised.

He nodded and held out his hand. She laid the spoons in his palm, and her fingers brushed against his, the sensation warm and inviting. Quickly, she removed her hand, and when she looked up at him, he grinned.

"Nothing to be embarrassed about," he said. He leaned over the bar and whispered, "I felt it, too."

Ruth blushed. Sean stood back up, rapped the spoons on the bar, and winked at her, then joined the two men for an impromptu music session. One removed a fiddle from his case, and the other had a bodhran, a big drum with a leather cover. Sean took the spoons in his right hand, placing them back to back between his fingers.

Ruth stayed close to the bar, ready to serve drinks as needed, but she came out from behind it and climbed up on a stool so she could get a better look. Mesmerized, she watched as Sean clicked the spoons between the top of his left thigh and his left hand, while his right foot tapped along in rhythm.

Fun. It was the only word that could describe it, hanging out in an Irish pub on a weekday afternoon, watching three men make music. She would later describe it as one of the most enjoyable weekday afternoons of her life.

Sean looked over at her and winked, and she returned the smile. She could not deny the physical attraction she felt for him. It was like the beat of a jungle drum, and it had awakened something very primitive in her that she had not known existed in real life. It was something she had written about and daydreamed about, but not something she'd ever known.

The musicians played for an hour, until the music and general bonhomie were interrupted by the front door of the pub banging open and the postman barreling through, breathless.

"Sean!" he shouted. "It's Mackie!"

Without a word or even a question, Sean jumped up and bolted from the pub, his spoons clattering to the floor.

# CHAPTER SEVENTEEN

Sean was out of the van like a flash, before the postman had even shifted it into park. Pushing through the front door of the house, all sorts of thoughts raced through his mind. His legs felt like lead.

"Mackie!" he shouted, hoping what the postman had told him wasn't true. He willed his uncle to respond, but was met with silence. He bounded down the hall to the back of the house, toward the kitchen, where Mackie could always be found.

The door to the kitchen opened and the local GP, a man not much older than Sean, faced him.

"I'm sorry, Sean," he started.

But Sean shoved past him and pulled up short

just inside the kitchen when he caught sight of his uncle. Mackie sat slumped in his favorite chair by the hearth, the fire long gone to ashes. He looked as if he were asleep.

"No," Sean whispered, still not quite believing it. He fell into the chair on the other side of the fire, across from Mackie, as he had so many evenings before.

"When?" he asked, looking over at the doctor.

The doctor shook his head. "Most likely sometime last night."

Suddenly riddled with guilt, Sean thought of all the things he had done that day, from whistling while making breakfast to taking a long, fresh walk in the early afternoon, to that overall good feeling he'd had playing the spoons that afternoon with Ruth minding the bar. Worst of all, he'd been in the orchard earlier that morning, but he never stopped in to see his uncle because he knew he didn't get up that early. And all that time, the man had been sitting in his chair, dead.

He hung his head and leaned his elbows on his knees.

The doctor set his black leather bag on the kitchen table.

"I know it has come as a shock, but Mackie was

closer to ninety than he was to eighty," the doctor started.

Sean shrugged. "So?" What did that mean? That the loss was any less because Mackie was old?

"Meaning he had a good life," the doctor replied. "You know as well as I that all he talked about was Carmel. If anything, take comfort in the fact that he is with her once again."

Sean looked up and said in a low voice, "It's for my own selfish reasons that I want him here."

"Of course," the doctor conceded. "I've made arrangements for the body to be picked up."

"He's not a body, he's Mackie," Sean growled.

The doctor shrugged, picked up his bag, and exited the room. The postman came in, as had Mackie's dog, Sparky, taking advantage of the open front door. The dog ran around the kitchen, barking, and then came to an abrupt halt in front of Mackie. He sat down and howled.

The postman handed Sean a tumbler of whiskey.

"I don't drink," Sean reminded him.

"Never mind that, you've had a shock," Moss said, forcing the glass of amber liquid into Sean's hand.

He drained it in one gulp. The alcohol burned

on the way down. He wiped his mouth on the back of his hand.

"I need to ring my brothers," Sean said absent-mindedly.

"What about the dog?" Moss asked. "You can't leave him here."

"I can't take him to the pub. He doesn't get on with my dog," Sean said, sighing as he studied the vertically challenged terrier. He was an older dog, and surly on the best of days.

"I suppose I could take him," the postman offered. "He knows me, at least."

"Thank you," Sean said. He waved off Moss's offer of any additional help, preferring to be alone with his uncle until the undertaker arrived.

SEAN HAD DECLINED all offers of a lift back to the pub, deciding he'd walk back. His emotions had balled up and sprung free. Walking would help. The village was only a few miles. Besides, his recent ancestors had walked or ridden bikes just about everywhere. The cool night air would clear his head.

Mackie was dead. How could that be? All this

time, since Carmel's death, Sean had thought he was helping his uncle. Looking after him, spending time with him, taking him to his doctor's appointments. But with his death, Sean realized it had been his uncle who was looking after him. He had depended on Mackie, not the other way around.

He paused at the side of the road, looking at the ditch but not seeing anything, because it had gone dark. Bending over, he laid his hands on his thighs and gasped.

It was the end of an era. They were all gone now. His parents, his aunts, his uncles. The generation that had acted as a shield between him and death was no longer there. With his uncle died the old ways, the traditions, the memories. He stood back up and drew in a deep breath, trying to stem the tears that threatened to flow. Agitation, restlessness, and feelings he had no name for gripped him, coursing through him and propelling him faster toward his own home, his rooms above the pub.

The village came into view in the distance, lights twinkling from the houses that lined the main street. He broke into a run.

Ruth came to mind. The red hair. The alabaster skin. Those green eyes. That smile. That laugh. She had stirred something within him he'd thought was long dead.

The fragility of life was heavy on his mind. As were other thoughts, such as missed opportunities.

Fueled by his grief, he ran until his chest burned. He had a plan. He was going to Ruth and he was going to take her in his arms. He planned to kiss her in a way he'd wanted to for a long time. There'd be no holding back. By the time he was finished kissing her, there would be no doubt on her part as to how he felt about her.

He didn't care if the pub was packed to the rafters, or if the villagers gossiped about it for days. The thought of taking that flame-haired American in his arms urged him onward.

When he reached the door of the pub, he pushed through it. His eyes scanned the crowded interior for Ruth. She stood behind the bar with Marie. Marie was giving out to someone, and Ruth was pouring a pint, looking like she belonged there, like it was her natural setting.

She turned in his direction, and as soon as her eyes met his, her smile disappeared. Setting the pint glass down, she came out from behind the bar, wiping her hands on a towel.

He was going to go for it before he lost his nerve. He went toward her and was relieved when she started coming toward him. But she halted and turned her head away. Sean frowned. His eyes followed her gaze, and he stopped in his tracks.

Him. That fella from Cork. He carried a tray with dirty pint glasses on it.

Of all things, Sean had not expected this.

"What's he doing?" Sean asked, sounding harsher than he had intended.

"Helping out," Ruth replied quickly. "He stopped by, but I didn't want to leave Marie alone, and Paul said he'd stay and lend a hand."

She reached out for Sean, but he took a step back. "How are you?" she asked quietly. There was tenderness in her face.

He forced a mask of self-control, an effort that was nothing short of Herculean. "I'm fine," he said abruptly. "Look, thanks for your help, but I can manage now."

Ruth started to protest, but they were interrupted by Paul.

"I'm starting to get the hang of this," said the interloper with a smile.

Sean narrowed his eyes at him.

Ruth looked from one to the other. "Sean, this is Paul Reilly. Paul, this is Sean Hughes."

For a moment, Sean regarded him warily. Then Paul threw out his hand. "Hey, mate, sorry for your loss."

"Thanks," Sean said, reluctantly shaking his hand. He turned to Ruth. "Look, it's all good. I appreciate your help, but I'm here now and I don't want to interrupt your plans."

Without waiting for an answer, Sean swept past them, his hand touching Ruth's arm lightly.

# CHAPTER EIGHTEEN

A sign was placed in the front window of the pub, stating that it would remain closed for three days out of respect for Mackie.

Sean had remained distant after he'd returned from Mackie's, and Ruth chalked it up to shock and grief. She had waited for Sean to return but Paul had shown up, bringing the first three chapters of the novel he'd written. As much as Ruth had wanted to help Paul, she wanted to be alone with Sean. But the opportunity never presented itself.

She had settled in a back corner of the pub with Paul, giving him recommendations on books on the craft of writing. Trying not to be rude, Ruth took his sample chapters and promised to read them.

Once Paul was gone, she headed upstairs to find that Sean had already gone to bed.

Sean hadn't been there at breakfast and Ruth assumed he was at Mackie's or the orchard or both. Ruth operated quietly upstairs, trying to make herself useful. With the pub closed, there really wasn't much for her to do. She could have gone sightseeing, but she didn't want to leave Sean. Couldn't leave him. She more or less left him to himself, but he hardly moved from his chair in front of the range. From time to time he changed his position, stretching his legs out and putting his feet up, or leaning forward, resting his elbows on his knees.

She handed him a plated ham sandwich and a cup of hot, strong tea, and he looked up at her, searching her face. It was then that she saw the depths of his grief and sadness, and something tugged at her heart.

She fixed herself a cup of tea and a sandwich for herself, then sat across from him. She started to say something, then cleared her throat and tried again. "Will there be a service?"

He looked at her as if it were the first time he was seeing her. "Yes. He'll be waked from his home tonight and tomorrow. He'll be removed to the church tomorrow night, and his funeral Mass will be Thursday morning."

"Is there anything I can do?" She searched his face. "I'd like to help."

"Would you?" he asked.

She nodded.

"You could help Marie out at the house during the wake. There'll be tea and sandwiches and cake and that sort of thing."

"At the wake?" she questioned.

He nodded and explained, "It's how things are done here."

"Okay."

He stammered, "I-I mean, you don't have to if you don't want to."

Unable to resist, she reached out and laid her hand on his arm. "Please, let me."

He nodded and resumed staring into space.

MARIE, carrying two armloads of pies and cakes, directed operations from the kitchen of Mackie's farmhouse. She supervised the rearranging of furniture to accommodate the impending arrival of mourners. Moss and another fella Ruth did not know by name but knew by sight, pushed the table up against the wall. Two of Mackie's neighbors from the passageway were lining chairs against the wall and around the hearth. Mackie would be laid out in the front room, or the "good room," as Marie referred to it. Mackie was arriving from the undertakers' later in the afternoon. The other sitting room was set up, as well.

Ruth watched in awe as a steady stream of neighbors, friends, and villagers came in, sympathized, and dropped off cakes, pies, and chairs. Sean arrived with someone's trailer hitched to his car, loaded with all the chairs from the pub. She raised her eyebrows, wondering how many people they were expecting.

"How many kettles and teapots do we have?" Marie asked.

Ruth did a quick count. "We have four electric kettles, one on the range, and three teapots."

Marie nodded. "That should be enough." She addressed Sean's two sisters-in-law, who had arrived ready to help.

"Peggy, set out all the dishes and teacups on the table. Dorothy, gather the silverware."

"I've brought more dishes from the pub," Sean said.

Marie held a bottle of furniture polish and a clean cloth in her hand. She looked to Ruth. "Would you mind polishing the furniture in the good room? We'll want it ready by the time Mackie arrives."

"I'd be happy to," Ruth replied. She wanted to help. She was grateful that they let her, instead of shutting her out as a foreigner or someone who didn't belong. She supposed that after four weeks of boarding at Sean's pub, the locals had gotten used to her. It gave her a sense of belonging in that tight-knit group that she hadn't ever felt to that degree before.

She headed down the hall toward the front of the farmhouse. The good room was done up in a floral carpet and striped wallpaper, and in the center was a brown-and-white tiled fireplace. Built-in cabinets lined the wall, one side filled with books and the other side with various forms of crystal glasses and fine china. Ruth thought it was a lovely room. She could imagine people entertaining there.

Peggy appeared in the doorway, dragging a canister vacuum behind her. "Ruth? Marie wondered if you might give the room a quick hoovering?"

Ruth nodded. "Sure, no problem."

Peggy was married to one of Sean's older brothers, Connor, and they lived down in Cork. They had two sons who had just started primary school.

"It's very kind of you to do this," Peggy said.

Ruth smiled. She had taken an instant liking to Peggy.

"It's the least I can do, for all that Sean has done for me."

Peggy looked at her. "Sean's a great guy. We're all hoping he finds a nice girl to settle down with. He loves kids, and he should have his own."

"Er . . . okay," Ruth said.

"We just don't want to see him hurt again," Peggy said.

"No, of course not," Ruth replied. What else could she say?

"What do you think about Sean?"

Ruth froze, not expecting such a direct question. Luckily, she was prevented from answering by the arrival of Dorothy in the room, who wore a sour expression and eyed Ruth suspiciously. Dorothy was married to the other brother, Tommy, and they lived up in Galway with their baby daughter.

"I told Marie that I would give this room a good cleaning," Dorothy said.

"I'm almost finished," Ruth said.

"It should have been done by someone in the family," Dorothy said, before stomping back off to the kitchen.

Ruth felt her face go red, but Peggy laughed.

"Pay no mind to her. More territorial than a Jack Russell!"

Ruth smiled but still felt unsure.

Peggy reassured her, "If Sean didn't want you here, you wouldn't be here."

Ruth wondered about that.

SEAN FELT the best way to deal with Mackie's death was to keep busy. He spent the morning bringing up chairs to the farmhouse and moving furniture, getting ready for the company that would descend later that night and over the course of the next two days. He still couldn't believe his uncle was gone. Every time he glanced at Mackie's empty chair, a lump formed in his throat.

The other distraction proved to be Ruth. It was hard not to be aware that she was nearby in his general sphere. It was also hard not to be touched that she was helping out. The previous night, he'd planned on taking Ruth in his arms, but the appearance of the Cork man had taken care of that. He didn't blame the man for his attraction to Ruth. But it left him wondering how Ruth felt about the other fella. Finally, seeing the state he was in, Marie had rung the bell and closed the pub. He'd gone upstairs and gone straight to his room. For a long time, he lay in the dark going back and forth between the loss of his uncle and his feelings for Ruth.

He carried two chairs, one on each arm, into the good sitting room. As he entered, he caught Ruth pushing the hoover around, concentrating on her task. For a split second, he had a wistful glimpse into his own future, a possible future with her at his side. The two of them, working as a team. But then Paul's face appeared in his mind, and Sean could practically feel himself baring his teeth.

As he set the chairs down, Ruth noticed him and straightened up, the long arm of the canister in her hand. She smiled warmly at him.

Dorothy stuck her head in the door. She eyed Ruth, then turned back to Sean. "The family is going to town for a meal."

Sean was embarrassed. Sometimes, his sister-in-law could be a wagon. "Ruth, will you come with us to dinner?" He ignored the look on Dorothy's face.

Ruth shook her head. "No, thanks. But you should go."

Reluctantly, he left her.

# CHAPTER NINETEEN

Ruth kept busy in the kitchen. Under Marie's direction, there were the wares to be laid out: napkins, plates, and utensils. She and Peggy made sandwiches, cut them into quarters, laid them out on trays, and wrapped them in cling wrap. There was turkey and stuffing with mayo, ham, and coleslaw with a thin slice of tomato.

Peggy handed Ruth a turkey sandwich. "You'll need to keep your strength up for later," she said with a smile.

Ruth took it from her gratefully, her stomach growling.

"Come on, let's sit down for a minute and have a cuppa."

They pulled out two chairs at the end of the table. Peggy poured tea into two mugs, then grabbed two plates and put a slice of cake and a piece of apple tart with a generous dollop of cream on each.

Dorothy walked by with her nose in the air, and Peggy rolled her eyes.

"Pay no attention to her. She's loyal to a fault and thinks it's her job to protect the family."

Ruth didn't say anything, figuring she wasn't part of the inside loop, and it wasn't her place to voice an opinion on the matter.

Peggy spoke about her kids and her husband, and Ruth was relieved that she had someone to talk to, as she had begun to feel a little out of place.

Sean walked into the kitchen and approached Ruth and Peggy, smiling.

"A cup of tea? Thanks, Peggy, I don't want our guest here thinking we wouldn't feed her," Sean said, winking at Ruth.

Without him asking, Peggy poured him a mug of tea and handed it to him. "You look like you could use something stronger, but this will have to do for now."

"Thanks, mate," Sean said, taking the mug from her, pouring in a bit of milk from a pitcher, and spooning in some sugar.

"Calvin is on his way," one of Sean's brothers

yelled from the front door. Sean set his cup down, stood up, and exited the front of the house.

Unsure of what to do, Ruth followed everyone else outside. A long black hearse came into sight at the end of the passage, and she was moved by the respectful silence that accompanied it. As it neared, Ruth saw the pine coffin with brass fixtures through the windows.

Sean and his brothers stood in the first row. Both his brothers were friendly, and tall and dark-haired like Sean. The wives were at their husbands' sides, and Ruth stayed behind, knowing her place. Sean glanced back at her, and she gave him a reassuring smile.

The coffin was removed from the hearse by Calvin and an assistant, and set on a trolley. With the undertaker providing direction, Sean, his brothers, and a few neighbors lifted it from the trolley and carried it into the front room of the farmhouse. Sean's face was a stoic mask of sorrow as he escorted his late uncle's remains into the house. Peggy, Dorothy, and Marie followed them in, followed by the neighbors, and that left Ruth bringing up the rear.

When the coffin was set up in the front parlor, the undertaker removed the lid, and Sean and his brothers stood beside it, gazing down at their late uncle. All three of them made the sign of the cross and said a few silent prayers. Following the rest of mourners, Ruth approached the dead man, thinking about the brief conversations they'd had in the pub. She said a silent prayer, then stepped back, catching a nod from Marie to follow her back to the kitchen. She stole a glance at Sean, whose face was awash with grief. Her heart tugged at the sight of him. More than anything, she wanted to take him in her arms and comfort him.

A STEADY STREAM OF FAMILY, neighbors, and villagers trickled in after seven. It wasn't long before the seats in the kitchen, the back parlor, and the front parlor began to fill up. Ruth was busy filling the kettles and making pots of tea. She circled the room with a teapot, pouring tea and passing along milk and sugar. Sandwiches and desserts were lined up on the kitchen table. She had counted no less than twenty tarts and ten different kinds of cakes. The mourners reminisced. Out of the corner of her eye, she watched Sean, commiserating with other people and sharing a joke or a laugh, presumably about his uncle. But beneath the forced joviality was a sadness that engulfed him. She wished she could help him. She figured the best way to do that was to be as unobtrusive as possible.

After a few hours, Ruth turned her back on the emotional display and busied herself at the sink, washing what seemed to be an endless flow of plates, cups, saucers, and spoons. She put them in a drying rack, and Peggy dried as she washed. She tried not to think of her aching leg. She was up to her wrists in dishwater when she felt a strong hand on her shoulder, and before she even turned around, she knew who it was. There was only one touch that affected her that way, making her knees weak and her legs turn to jelly. She looked up into the face of Sean.

"Have you sat at all tonight?" he asked, concern flooding his voice. His eyes were full of tenderness as they searched her face.

She blew a stray hair out of her line of vision, as her hands were wet. "I will. I'm almost finished."

"Leave them and sit, both of you," Sean instructed.

Peggy didn't have to be told twice. She set the dishtowel down on the counter and went and sat next to her husband, running her hand along his back.

Sean took the dishtowel, and when Ruth took her hands out of the soapy water, he began to dry them. Ruth watched his face intently as he focused on his task, tenderly drying each one of her fingers and then her palms. His touch resonated up her arms and through her body, like a live wire.

When he finished, he looked at her, still holding her hands. "You're trembling, Ruth Davenport."

She swallowed hard and pulled her hands away, embarrassed. "I'm just tired."

He nodded. "Come here and sit down."

She followed him to two chairs by the fire, and with relief, sat down.

"I'll be right back," he said with a smile.

He went to the table laden with food and made two plates. He poured two mugs of tea and, balancing it all with a laugh, he carried his armload back over to Ruth. He occupied the seat next to her and handed her one of the plates and a mug of tea.

"Thank you," she said.

"No, it should be me who's thanking you," he said.

She shrugged and gave a little laugh. "After all you've done for me since I've landed on your doorstep, it's the least I could do."

He regarded her for a moment and then broke into a warm smile.

They ate and drank in companionable silence. Ruth thought that this was what it would be like to be in a relationship where you didn't need to fill the void with constant chirping, where you could be there for one another during times of sorrow. This is what it would be like, she thought, to have that devastating chemistry, the companionship, and basically the whole package. It was what Majella had talked about.

Sean leaned toward her but said nothing, and Ruth felt as if this moment was oddly intimate, a space that belonged only to the two of them. If only, she thought wistfully.

Somebody on the other side of the kitchen called for music, and it wasn't long before an impromptu trad session broke out. Sean finished his tart and took their plates to the sink. Two fiddles were produced, as well as a bodhran, a tin whistle, and an accordion, which someone referred to as a concertina. Sean asked Ruth if she would mind holding his mug of tea, then he procured a set of spoons. The amateur musicians started some Irish verse, and Sean clacked his spoons in time with the music. Ruth watched as they played song after song, completely mesmerized.

There was a change in the atmosphere not unlike when her sister, Nicole, arrived somewhere. First, Ruth noticed Sean had stopped playing his spoons. His gaze was fixed on something just behind her. Slowly and as unobtrusively as possible, she turned her head in the direction in which he stared. In the doorway stood a woman about the same age as Ruth. She was tall, with hair the color of honey and cornflower-blue eyes. She appeared to hesitate, but she also exuded an air of confidence Ruth envied. Unable to help it, her gaze drifted to the woman's athletic legs, thinking she must be a runner of some kind.

Sean stood up, laying the spoons on the chair he'd just vacated.

Peggy picked up the spoons and sat down in Sean's vacated seat. She whispered, "She's got a lot of brass, showing up here."

Ruth looked at her, uncomprehending.

Peggy grimaced. "Brid."

"Oh," Ruth said knowingly. She kept her eyes on them.

"Sean," Brid said, searching his face.

"Brid," he said. His face showed no emotion. With his hand on her elbow, Sean guided his former fiancée away from the kitchen full of people.

Ruth stared at the empty space he'd left behind. Suddenly, she felt bereft.

People began to stand up, pushing their chairs back and carrying empty mugs and plates to the sink. Looking out the window, Ruth noted it had gone dark. She glanced at the clock above the mantel and was surprised to see it was almost eleven. And to think they would do all this again tomorrow.

To take her mind off of Sean, she helped Marie and Peggy put cling wrap on all the food, storing what was perishable in the refrigerator and leaving the rest of it on the table. They washed and dried the rest of the dishes, and once all the ware was cleaned and put away, the three of them wiped down the tables and chairs and swept the floor.

Sean reappeared in the kitchen, looking distracted. "Ruth, where is your coat?"

"In the back hall," she replied.

"Connor and Peggy will give you a lift back to the pub," he said absently.

"What about you?" she asked, her heart sinking.

He shook his head. "I'll stay here tonight." He paused and then added, "It's an old custom for someone to sit with the dead overnight, so that's what I'll be doing."

"Oh," she said. Tentatively, she asked, "Did you want some company?"

He shook his head. "Thank you, but no."

"I don't mind," she said.

"No, really. You've done enough. What I would

like you to do is go back to the house and get a good night's sleep."

She was nodding, but she would have preferred to stay, just to be near him. "Is there anything else I can do?"

He shook his head. "No." He paused as if struggling to say something. He looked down at his feet for a moment. "Look, we've to do this all again tomorrow, and I can't ask or expect you to make tea and wash dishes for people you don't even know."

"I don't mind."

"Wouldn't you rather go sightseeing for the day? You could take my car," he suggested.

"I really don't mind," she insisted.

"It just seems wrong to ask you to do all this."

"It's not a problem," she said.

He relented. "All right, then. I'll see you at some point tomorrow."

She nodded, resisting the urge to stand on her tiptoes and kiss him good night or place her hand alongside his cheek. Instead, she laid her hand on his arm. "Good night, Sean."

As she walked down the narrow hall, she caught sight of Brid parked on the sofa in the front room. Ruth's heart sank.

~

ON THE MORNING of the funeral, Ruth worried about her outfit. She had not brought anything in somber colors except a black cardigan sweater, which she paired with a white dress with black and gray flowers on it. She didn't think it was funereal enough. Entering the kitchen, she was just about to ask Sean his opinion when she did a double take.

Sean stood before her wearing suit pants, a crisp white shirt, and a navy-blue tie. His suit coat hung over the back of a chair. Ruth's mouth fell open when she saw that his beard and mustache were gone. His clean-shaven face featured prominent cheekbones and a strong jaw. She stared for a good minute before finally getting out, "What happened to your beard?" She would miss that beard, but she liked the new look, as well. It would just take some getting used to.

He shrugged and explained, "Mackie was always after me to get rid of it. I thought today was as good a day as any, if only to show my respect."

"That's nice."

"You were going to ask me something?" he asked.

"It's my dress; I don't think it's black enough," she said anxiously. She wasn't sure what the custom was and she certainly didn't want to offend any of the villagers.

Sean was about to say something but hesitated. "You look fine."

They stood there for a moment, neither saying anything.

Finally, Ruth said, "I'll just grab my purse." And she disappeared back to her bedroom.

~

IT HAD BEEN A LONG DAY, and Ruth was exhausted. After the funeral and the luncheon at a hotel in the next village, Sean had opened the pub. There was a lot of spillover from the funeral. As the pub had been closed a few days, it seemed the natural place to gather to continue to mourn Mackie. She bypassed the noisy pub and headed toward the staircase behind the bar. Her plans included a nice long soak in the tub, a hot cup of tea, and a jar for the foot of the bed.

She hadn't said anything on the way home. Conflicted thoughts boomeranged around the inside of her head until she thought it was going to burst. She had begun to see Sean in a new light. And it was a light she wasn't so sure about.

From the moment she'd met him, she'd thought he was handsome, albeit in a way that didn't classify as her "type." But now something new had transpired. There had been a sudden shift, and it had knocked Ruth sideways. Had it been there all along? In the beginning, even though she often thought he was making fun of her, he'd been kind in allowing her to stay. At the time, she had chalked it up to the legendary Irish hospitality she'd heard so much about. But then as time went on, and she and Sean drove all over the country in the name of research and sightseeing, she'd realized she enjoyed the time she spent with him. It had gotten to the point where she looked forward more to the drives than the destinations.

Ruth couldn't deny her growing, devastating attraction to Sean. And she was someone who firmly believed that there either was chemistry between a couple, or there wasn't. It wasn't something that could be forced or faked. If the spark was there, then it needed to be cultivated. However, as much as she felt attracted to the Irish publican, she wasn't so sure he felt the same way about her. Sometimes she thought she caught Sean looking at her the way one of her male characters would look at the heroine in her books. It was a look that said she was his and no one else's. But then sometimes, Sean seemed to think she was a pain in the neck.

And there was another problem. She had fallen in love with Ireland. It had been hard not to: lush, green, hilly pastures hedged by ancient stone walls. The friendly people and the small local parish where everyone was welcome. And the laid-back rural lifestyle. She loved it to the point where she could see herself living there, and that had never been part of the plan.

She swallowed hard, thinking Ireland wasn't the only thing she'd fallen in love with on this trip.

She chastised herself on these far-flung ideas. Look where it had gotten her the last time, with her crush now dating her sister, because Ruth had misread the signs and the cues along the way. Here she was, a comfortably successful romance writer, and she couldn't tell the difference between flirting and friendliness. The irony was not lost on her. It was time to go back to the drawing board or at the very least, change genres. Maybe she should write crime fiction or cozy mysteries instead.

Ruth stood at the foot of the staircase and looked up to the top. Her leg throbbed, and the top of the stairs seemed a very long way away.

Sighing, she told herself that she would take it one step at a time. She reminded herself of the rewards at the top: peace and quiet, a hot bath, and a nice, comfy bed.

"Ruth, are you all right?" Sean asked from behind her, startling her.

She turned to look up at him, his eyes glittering in the dim light of the hall.

"I . . . I . . ." she started, then gave up. Exhaustion overwhelmed her.

"Your leg is bothering you," he said. It was not a question.

Without a word, he scooped her up, gathering her in his arms and catching her by surprise.

"Oh!" she said.

Effortlessly, he stepped onto the staircase.

"Oh, no, Sean, I'm too heavy," she protested. "I'll break your back."

He laughed, beginning the ascent up the staircase. "My back will be grand; you'll see."

He smelled wonderful, and it took all of Ruth's self-control not to lay her head on his chest. He set her down gently on the landing at the top. They stood for a moment in the gathering darkness.

Stepping closer, Sean reached out for her and said in a low voice, "Ruth."

Her heartbeat accelerated in anticipation. She searched his face. Everything felt suspended as he leaned toward her, and Ruth parted her lips, her eyes never leaving his.

From below, the door from the bar swung open, and Marie yelled, "Sean!"

Abruptly, Sean pulled away from her, and for a

moment Ruth thought she had only imagined he was going to kiss her.

"Yes, Marie, what is it?" Sean asked, his voice tight.

"There's someone here to see the Yank."

Ruth placed both hands on her chest and mouthed, "Me?"

Sean grinned. "Will I carry you back down?" he asked. She laughed.

He reached for her hand and gave it a squeeze, and Ruth looked up at him, smiling. She followed him down the staircase carefully, wondering who could be looking for her. A little pit of dread formed in her stomach. She hoped it wasn't Paul. She wanted to help him, but tonight she was exhausted and she just wanted to be alone with Sean.

But by the time she reached the bottom of the staircase, in that moment before she even slipped through the doorway to the bar, she became aware of an all-too-familiar feeling. The usually noisy pub had become subdued. And when Sean held the door open for her, Ruth's suspicions were confirmed.

Nicole had landed in Ireland in all her usual glory.

# CHAPTER TWENTY

"Ruth!" Nicole squealed when she caught sight of her sister.

Ruth slowly advanced, thinking how quickly this trip had turned into a nightmare. A quick look told her that her sister was alone, and Ruth knew that didn't bode well for her.

Her sister threw her arms around her and hugged her. Ruth remained wooden. Sean watched the pair of them, smiling, working that toothpick in his mouth, and Ruth's heart turned cold; she knew she couldn't compete with her sister. Nicole would hijack this country, too. The thought of Sean and Nicole together made Ruth's stomach revolt.

Nicole chittered on, oblivious to Ruth's discomfort.

"What are you doing here?" Ruth finally managed to ask.

"Well," Nicole started, tucking a strand of blonde hair behind her ear. "Six weeks is a long time! I missed you, and I finally told Dad I would come over and see for myself what you were up to." She paused and spread her arms wide. "And here I am!"

"Yes, here you are," Ruth said, her words thick in her mouth, as if she'd been overmedicated. After a moment, she asked, "Is Dad all right?"

Nicole waved a hand away. "Dad's fine. He just wants to know what's going on over here."

"I told you; I'm working. Other than that, nothing much. It's a nice country," Ruth said. Wow, she sounded like she had a flat affect. Sean was looking at her strangely. "How long are you staying?"

Nicole looped her arm through Ruth's, almost knocking her off balance. "I'm staying as long as you are!"

Ruth wanted to throw up. Couldn't she just have one thing that was hers alone? Like this country? She was ashamed of how she felt. She looked at Sean again and felt all hope was lost. "Oh, I'm sorry. Sean, this is my sister, Nicole. Nicole, this is

Sean. He owns this pub. I've been staying in one of the rooms upstairs."

Nicole smiled at him and winked at Ruth. "You've gone and got yourself a man! And a fine-looking one at that!"

Sean shuffled his feet and looked at the ground. Ruth was mortified. "Will you shut up, Nicole? It's nothing like that. He just helped me out when I was in trouble."

Sean was uncharacteristically silent.

"Is your leg bothering you, Ruth?" Nicole asked sympathetically. "You always get cranky when your leg acts up."

"I'm not cranky," Ruth said through clenched teeth. "Where are you staying?"

Nicole smiled patiently, as if Ruth were a small child or something. "Well, I was hoping to stay with you."

"You can't stay here; there's no room," Ruth said.

Sean interrupted. "Of course she can," he said in a quiet voice. "She can have the room next to yours."

Ruth thought of the three of them upstairs together, and the tears threatened. "I'm so sorry. I'm just tired. Nicole, I'll see you in the morning." As fast as she was physically able, Ruth bolted from the pub to her room upstairs.

~

SEAN HAD NEVER SEEN a personality change come over anyone so instantly as it had come over Ruth when her sister showed up. He had to admit Nicole's timing had not been perfect, as he had been about to lay a kiss on Ruth's lips. He'd thought she had wanted him to, but then she'd downplayed their relationship in front of her own sister. She made it sound like she didn't feel at all the way he felt about her.

After Ruth left the room, he made the sister a drink and told her to park herself on a stool at the bar.

"She didn't look very happy to see me," Nicole said. She looked nervously around the pub. She had the attention of every man there. She was foreign. And she was beautiful. When she reached into her purse for some money, Sean shook his head.

"This one's on me," he said.

"Thank you," she said.

He lifted his glass of soda water. "Cheers. And welcome to Ireland."

She forced a smile and sipped her drink. Her

suitcase remained at her feet. She fidgeted with the stem of her glass, and he felt sorry for her.

"What's the plan while you're in Ireland?" he asked, twirling the toothpick in his mouth.

She shrugged. "I really don't know. I had hoped to stay with Ruth for the rest of her time here. I know she's working, but I thought we might do a bit of sightseeing and spend some time together. Maybe that's not such a good idea."

Sean leaned on the bar. "She's had a busy couple of days. She may just be tired."

Nicole nodded knowingly. "She can't overdo it. When she gets tired or stressed, her leg really starts to bother her."

"I figured that," he said. "You must be famished. We don't serve food, but I could whip you up a sandwich."

"That would be so kind," she said.

He ran upstairs to his kitchen, took a few things out of the fridge, and made her a ham-and-cheese sandwich on brown bread. He pulled a bag of crisps from the box underneath the cabinet. His plan was to feed her and enquire as discreetly as possible about Ruth.

When he returned to the bar, two lads he played hurling with stood on either side of Nicole, chatting her up. So much for the planned subterfuge, he thought.

He smiled as he set down the plate and the bag of crisps in front of her.

“Thank you so much,” she said. “I’m starved.”

She returned her attention to the two men at her side.

Nicole wilted quickly after she finished eating, yawning repeatedly. She bid her would-be suitors good night.

Sean showed her the way to her room, pointing out the bathroom at the other end of the hall. She nodded, her face pale and circles under her eyes. He noticed she wore jeans and a turtleneck. She obviously didn’t share her sister’s love of frocks and flowers.

Where Ruth was red-haired and green-eyed, Nicole had long blonde hair with blue eyes. She was a beautiful woman, but in Sean’s opinion, she couldn’t hold a candle to Ruth.

After he carried her suitcase into the room, he asked her if she needed anything, and when she said no, he closed the door softly behind him.

He paused at Ruth’s door, standing for a moment outside it, tempted to knock and see if she was all right. But no light shone from beneath the door.

He stared at that strip of darkness for a minute, then, restless, he moved on to his own room.

~

SEAN LOOKED for something to do. Anything. Anything to take his mind off of Mackie's death and distract him from the fact that Ruth wasn't there. His thoughts wandered toward the American, as they had been doing with increasing regularity. She'd taken her sister to Dublin yesterday. They were going to do some sightseeing and they would be returning at some point that day.

He *missed* her.

No floral dresses swirling past him. No flame-haired siren to gaze at. No scent of soft perfume floating by. No one to challenge him. No one to talk to.

He parked himself on a stool in front of the bar, his book of poetry open in front of him. There were only two patrons sitting at the other end of the bar, and he had just refilled their pint glasses.

"Sean?"

Brid.

He sighed, closing his book.

"I see you're still reading poetry," she said, now at his side.

"What can I do for you, Brid?" he asked, standing up from the stool and doing a quick visual check on his customers.

"I was hoping we could talk," she said. She placed her hand on his arm. But it no longer belonged there, and he shrugged her off.

"Talk about what?" he asked tightly.

She smiled. "What do you think? You and me, of course."

He shook his head. "No thanks, that ship has sailed."

"Please, Sean," she said.

"Five minutes, Brid," he said. He indicated with a nod that they should step outside. He'd didn't want the sad, sorry state of affairs that was his private life on display for the whole village.

He held the door open for her and followed her out. The two of them sat on the top of one of the picnic tables out front, staring at the village spread out before them. Before, when they'd been together, they used to sit outside like this, often after a match, his or hers, discussing the highlights. It seemed like a lifetime ago.

He didn't say anything, figuring since she was the one who wanted to talk, she could do the talking.

"You're looking well, Sean," she started.

"You, too, Brid," he said, arms folded across his chest, working the toothpick in his mouth.

A taxi pulled up in front of the pub, and out climbed Ruth and Nicole. Ruth, in a navy floral number, leaned in the window to pay the driver, and Sean watched, mesmerized. Brid looked back and forth between them.

Sean stood up from the table and Brid followed him.

The two sisters were huddled and laughing together, but Ruth stopped laughing when she laid eyes on him and Brid. The last thing in the world he wanted was for her to think he and Brid were back together. That would be disastrous.

"Look, Brid, I've got to get back inside," he said and added hastily, "I've got a pub to run." He ignored the wounded look on her face and sprinted into the pub, anxious to get away from her and his past.

BY THE TIME Ruth and Nicole had returned from Dublin, Ruth was exhausted. It had been a full day in the capital. And a lot of walking. She was looking forward to a quiet night in the pub with her sister. That was the plan until Sean rapped on her door and said, "That fella from Cork is downstairs looking for you."

Ruth rolled her eyes. She wished Paul hadn't shown up unannounced. Nicole sat on the bed, writing postcards to her friends. "Nicole, will you come downstairs with me?"

"I'm not going to be a third wheel with you and Paul," Nicole said. "You're not going to want your little sister tagging along on your date."

Ruth winced at the word "date." "He's just a friend. I'm helping him with his writing. Come on, let's just have a fun night out in an Irish pub."

Nicole laughed. "Didn't we do that last night?"

Ruth shook her head. "I suppose we did." Even Ruth had to admit she had had a great time with her sister. Her sister was a lot of fun and easy to travel with. "Nicole, you didn't come all this way to spend your time up in your room."

They ended up in a corner booth downstairs, as far away from the bar as possible. Paul slid into the booth next to Ruth.

He got right to the point. "I was in the area and thought I'd stop by," he said.

Ruth wondered about that. Tipperary wasn't exactly around the corner from Cork.

"Did you have a chance to read my sample chapters?" he asked.

Before Ruth could respond, Sean appeared at their table, asking if they'd like drinks. Paul ordered a round and Sean nodded, his expression unreadable. He didn't look at Ruth.

"He's kind of surly," Paul noted after he'd left.

"Sean?" Ruth asked, surprised. "He's not surly. He's very nice." Nicole raised an eyebrow ever so slightly.

Paul laughed. "He seems a bit rough around the edges. He's treating you all right?"

"Yes, of course," Ruth said.

"He makes a wicked fry-up," Nicole said.

Paul looked from Nicole and then back to Ruth. Lowering his voice, he asked, "He hasn't bothered you, has he?"

Ruth frowned, uncomprehending.

"You know, tried to take advantage of you?"

Ruth's hackles rose. "Of course not. He's been nothing but a gentleman."

Paul looked over to Sean and then back at Ruth. "I'm glad to hear that. But if he should ever bother you *that* way, let me know, and I'll have a word with him."

Ruth tried to envision Paul "having a word" with the publican. Sean'd clean up the parking lot with him. She looked over at the bar, where Sean stood at the cash register with his back to her. She *wished* he would bother her in that way.

Sean turned around and his eyes landed on hers. His face was a mask of turmoil.

Probably to do with Brid, she thought, and forced herself to look away.

"Actually, I have had a proper look at your material," Ruth said, forcing her thoughts off of Sean. She launched into a detailed account of her opinion on his writing, trying to help him as best as she could while trying not to think of Sean, who was so near yet so far away.

"WHY DON'T you tell Sean you're interested in him?" Nicole said later to Ruth as they sat in her room.

"What? Why don't you mind your own business?" Ruth snapped.

Nicole was startled into silence.

Ruth chastised herself. Why did she have to be so snarky toward her younger sister? Especially after the great time they'd had in Dublin.

"Sometimes I get the feeling you don't want me here," Nicole mumbled, sitting on the edge of the bed in Ruth's room.

Ruth sighed.

"I don't understand, Ruth. You run so hot and cold," her sister complained. "You're my only sister, and I want to be close to you, but you always keep me at arm's length."

Ruth hung her head and swallowed hard, ashamed of herself.

"Is it me? I know I can be a pain in the butt," Nicole said.

Ruth stared at her hands in her lap.

"Please, be honest with me and tell me what it is about me that bothers you."

Ruth regarded her sister for a moment, debating on whether honesty was the best policy in this case. She reached toward Nicole, took hold of her hand, and gave it a reassuring squeeze. "Nicole, the problem is something that can't be helped."

Her sister waited.

Ruth stared at the dated floral wallpaper, thinking it reminded her of the home of her long-dead grandparents. She found comfort in that.

"When you're around, I feel I don't stand a chance," she admitted.

Nicole frowned in confusion. "I don't understand."

Ruth sighed. "Nicole, men gravitate toward you because of how gorgeous you are, and sometimes I feel as if there is no one for me, that once they see you, they lose interest." Ruth felt shallow for admitting this.

"That's ridiculous!" Nicole said with a nervous laugh. She stared at her older sister for a moment and her eyes widened. "You're serious!"

Ruth nodded.

"Why on earth would you think that?" Nicole asked in disbelief. "Have you looked in the mirror yourself? You're beautiful! You have that red hair and flawless complexion that I would kill for."

It was Ruth's turn to look at her sister in wide-eyed disbelief.

Nicole was nodding her head. "It's true!"

"No, it's happened before. Men get to know me so they can get closer to you."

"I don't believe that," Nicole said. Then she added quietly, "I would never do that on purpose."

"I know," Ruth conceded.

"If you like someone, just tell me," Nicole said, "And I'll steer clear of him." She picked at imaginary lint on the quilted bedspread. "That's what sisters are for."

Nicole was right, thought Ruth. Sisters were supposed to have each other's backs.

"I had a crush on Steve," Ruth confessed, "and was just about to profess my feelings for him when he asked me if I would put in a good word with you."

Nicole scrunched up her nose. "Oh no. Why didn't you tell me?"

Ruth shrugged. "He was so into you, it didn't seem worth it. Besides, he was a nice guy."

"Well, let's just say that he certainly wasn't worth crying over."

"Oh no," Ruth said. "Did it not work out?"

Nicole shook her head. "It never seems to work out."

Ruth's face flooded with sympathy. "Are you okay?" Ruth was surprised that someone as beautiful as Nicole would have problems in her personal life. But there it was.

Her sister shrugged her shoulders. "It is what it is and all that. I can attract them, but I just can't keep them." There was a tremor in her sister's voice, and that crushed Ruth. But Nicole put on a brave face and laughed it off, forcing a cheeriness that belied her demeanor. "Oh well, what are you going to do? Anyway, what about that Irishman downstairs?"

"Sean?" Ruth asked, blinking.

Nicole rolled her eyes and giggled. "I wasn't referring to the man on the moon! Of course, Sean."

Ruth quickly shook her head to disabuse her

sister of any foolish notions. The same foolish notions she was currently deluding herself with, which she blamed on different scenery and being on vacation. Once back home, in the cold light of day, she would realize she had imagined all of it.

"Sean's very nice. He's been kind to me ever since I landed on his doorstep."

"Oh, I bet!" Nicole giggled.

"It isn't like that," Ruth protested.

"Don't fight it."

"Stop," Ruth said, playfully hitting her sister on the arm. Nicole fell amongst the pillows, laughing.

"He even gave you the best room in the house!"

It was Ruth's turn to giggle, and Nicole sat back up and laughed. "Seriously, my décor is brown and orange next door."

Ruth gave a pained smile. "It's been a long time since this place operated as a B & B."

"I'll say. Now, getting back to Sean. You must notice the way he looks at you?"

"I have. Like I'm some kind of crazy American."

Nicole shook her head. "Not at all. When you walk into a room, his face lights up."

Ruth blushed. "It does not!"

"It does. I've been watching him, and he can't take his eyes off of you."

"Nicole!"

"Listen, will I talk to him?" Nicole asked, lowering her voice.

Ruth became alarmed, fearing what her sister might actually mean.

Nicole continued. "Sean! You know, let him know you're interested?"

Ruth blanched. "Oh no! This isn't seventh grade recess! No, please do not say anything to him."

Nicole smiled.

Ruth grabbed both her hands and gripped them. "Seriously, Nicole, promise me you won't say anything to him about me or . . . us."

Nicole had stopped laughing. "I won't. I promise."

"Whew!" Ruth said, and she flopped back onto the bed. Nicole joined her, and soon the two of them started giggling again.

RUTH WALKED Nicole down to the bus stop at the end of the village.

"You don't have to leave," Ruth finally said. It was a mild day for the end of October. The blue sky was filled with big, white, fluffy clouds and the sunshine, although bright, was watery.

Nicole looked at her sister. "I do. Because as long as I'm here, you'll never get any time alone with Sean. And you won't be able to tell him how you feel." She looked around the little village and then back at Ruth. "And you must."

"I don't know," Ruth said, her confidence waning.

"You do know, Ruth," Nicole said firmly.

A Dublin coach, a newer, bright green bus, rolled into the bus stop.

"I'll be in Dublin for a few days—and if it works out between you and Sean, I'll go on ahead home," Nicole said. "Or you can catch up with me in Dublin. Either way works, although I'm rooting for the former."

Ruth wondered when her sister had become so mature.

The bus belched out a small plume of exhaust. The bus driver stepped down and took Nicole's one piece of luggage and stowed it in the compartment beneath the bus.

Nicole flung her arms around her sister and Ruth returned the hug.

"Be happy, Ruth," Nicole whispered in her ear.

When they pulled apart, Ruth had tears in her eyes. She took hold of her sister's hand and gave it a squeeze. "I'm so glad you came over, Nicole."

Ruth waited until the bus pulled out, waving at her sister. When it was gone from sight, she headed back to the pub. In her heart, she knew that Nicole was right. It was time to tell Sean how she felt about him. Now, if only she could find some courage.

# CHAPTER TWENTY-ONE

Sean watched as Ruth entered the pub.

"Did she get off all right?" he asked.

"Yes, she did," Ruth replied. "I'll meet up with her at the end of my trip."

With Nicole gone, they were alone again. The last time they'd been alone was at the top of the staircase when he'd been about to lay a kiss on her lips. He wondered if they could pick up where they left off. And then he wondered if Ruth even remembered that moment. He hoped so.

The afternoon was waning and the interior of the pub began to darken. It wouldn't be long before it would start filling up.

"Ruth—" he started.

"Sean—" she said simultaneously.

They both laughed.

"You go first," she said.

He swallowed hard and was about to ask her to go out with him that night. If she said yes, he'd close the pub.

He opened his mouth at the same time that Marie came through the door, followed by Calvin. Sean glanced at the clock. It was time for Marie's shift.

"Calvin, I don't appreciate you having a go at me," Marie said firmly.

Both Sean and Ruth were distracted by Marie's usually firm voice, which sounded tight. And hurt.

"How could you possibly think that?" Calvin asked, his own voice sounding wounded.

Marie spun around and confronted Calvin. "Because that's what ye do. Ye sit in here and drink all night and everything is funny to ye."

"Sometimes everything *is* funny," Calvin replied weakly.

"And sometimes it isn't," she said.

"Sometimes it isn't," he repeated.

Marie turned toward them and Sean didn't miss the look on her face: one of confusion and hesitation and surprise.

"This eejit has just asked me out."

When neither Sean nor Ruth responded, Marie added, "On a date!"

Sean clapped his hands. "Well, it's about time."

Marie looked surprised. "What do you mean?"

"Because I'm tired of looking at his lovesick mug from my side of the bar," Sean said.

Marie glanced at Calvin. "Is what he says true?"

Calvin nodded with a smile of serenity. "I'm afraid it is, Marie."

"Calvin, have ye completely lost your mind?" she asked. "We're shoving on to sixty!"

It was Calvin's turn to be offended. "So what? Aren't we entitled to a bit of happiness? Marie, I won't deny my feelings for you anymore. We're not getting any younger, and it would be nice to have a bit of happiness in the years we have left."

"I don't know what to say!"

"Just say yes!" He beamed.

Marie broke into a slow smile. "You stupid, old fool!"

Neither said a word at first and then finally, Marie said, "Yes, Calvin, I'll go out with ye."

"You will?" he asked, clearly shocked.

Marie rolled her eyes but laughed. "I just said I would, didn't I?"

Sean looked over at Ruth, who had a dreamy smile on her face.

"I'm glad that's finally sorted out, how about you?" he asked.

And as people streamed into the pub and his own idea of being alone with Ruth went out the window, Sean wondered if it would ever get sorted between them.

The pub business didn't let up until after dark. Sean became exasperated with the patrons. Pulling a pint annoyed him. Someone asking for lemon instead of lime irritated him. All he wanted was to be alone with Ruth. She hadn't said much but had retreated to her corner to work on her book. All evening, he looked over to her, anxious to be with her, but it never happened. He was just thinking he'd close the pub early when Brid arrived.

She stepped up to the bar and said, "I'd like to talk to you."

Sean glanced over at Ruth in the corner and saw that she was watching them.

"Can it wait until another time?" he asked.

Marie, who was standing next to him, interrupted and whispered to Sean, "Go and get her sorted out for once." Glancing at Ruth, she said, "So ye can move on with your life."

Signifying his displeasure with a loud sigh, he grabbed his coat and headed out the door with Brid.

They were no sooner out the door than he said, "Brid, what is it now?"

It was her turn to be exasperated. "Can we at least not do this in front of the pub? Can we go someplace private?"

He looked around, not really wanting to be alone with her. "Get in the car," he said.

The night sky was clear and dark with twinkling stars overhead. They drove through the village to the outskirts and ended up at the hurling pitch, parked in front of the concrete wall that surrounded it. Sean looked around, seeing no one, and was relieved.

"I wondered if you wanted to get back together?"

His eyes widened and his mouth went slack, causing his toothpick to fall out.

Seeing his expression, she said hurriedly, "We could start out slowly."

"Brid, I haven't had so much as a text from you in three years," he said.

"I know. At the time, I thought it was best to make a clean break," she said.

"You did say that when you left," he said, grateful that the sting from those words was no longer there. "But you left because you said you wanted to do some living before you settled down. And that living did not include me."

"And I also said that I hoped we could get back together again," she said.

"I do remember that, as well," he said. "But it's been three years. You can't have expected me to put my own life on hold and just be here waiting for you to come back." Although that was what he had done. He'd spent the first year staring at the door of the pub, willing her to walk through it. When she didn't, he'd gradually moved on with his own life. Such as it was.

Her lips thinned and her shoulders sagged. He hadn't forgot that: her ability to sulk. She was expert level, and it used to be on him to draw her out of it. Not today. Or tomorrow, for that matter.

"That is what you expected, isn't it?" he said, looking at her in disbelief. "That you could come back anytime, and we'd just pick up where we left off."

Shrugging, she looked straight ahead through the windshield at the hurling pitch. "Maybe."

Silence lingered between them.

"Since I've been back, I've done a lot of thinking," Brid said.

He looked at her. "Really? You only started thinking now since you've come back? I couldn't stop thinking from the moment you told me you were leaving."

They were both quiet for a while and eventually, Brid spoke. "I want to get back together. You're the one for me."

He had waited over three years for her to say those words to him. But now it was too late. The only thing Sean could think of was how he wished he could be that forthright with Ruth. And that's when he knew: he was totally over Brid. He hadn't known it at the time, but he had moved on with his life.

He wasn't going to get into it with Brid now. It was over.

"Brid, maybe you just associate me with Ballybeg. I wonder if you'd feel different about me if you were somewhere else, like Galway or Kilkenny or something."

"Oh, no I wouldn't," she protested.

He laughed but it was hollow. "Or Dublin."

Both went quiet.

"I am sorry, Sean," she said, just above a whisper.

"It's over, Brid," he said quietly. "Let me go."

For a while, neither said a word.

"Come on, I'll take you home," he said.

Once he dropped her off at her house, he headed

back toward the pub, thinking about his own fear of rejection at the hands of Ruth. It was getting late, and he'd try again tomorrow. He passed the pub, drove on, and soon found himself at Mackie's house.

Inside, he turned lights on and had a walk through, aware of how acutely he missed his uncle. The silence was loud and Mackie's absence had robbed the house of its personality. He made himself a cup of tea and sat down at the table, going over in his head what he would say to Ruth the next day. He fidgeted with his teacup, feeling restless. Finally, he had a thought and went to the front parlor where Carmel used to keep her stationery, wondering if it was even there anymore. After digging around in the cabinets of the bookcase, he found the stationery at the bottom of a pile. Excited, he headed back to the kitchen and found a pen in one of the drawers. He made himself another cup of tea, sat at the table, and began to write his thoughts down. He was going to write a letter to Ruth.

AFTER SEAN LEFT WITH BRID, speculation mounted among the pubgoers as to whether they were getting back together. It became so painful that Ruth closed her laptop and went upstairs. For a long while, she sat at the kitchen table and stared at the wall. She listened for Sean, waiting for him to come upstairs. She resolved not to go to bed until she spoke with him. Until she told him how she felt about him.

She made herself tea, practicing in her head what she was going to say. Eventually she heard Marie ring the bell downstairs, indicating the pub was closing. With relief, she knew Sean would be upstairs soon.

But it wasn't long after the closing bell when Marie popped her head around the door.

Ruth sat up straighter.

"Look, I'm going to lock up downstairs and head off," Marie said.

Ruth's heart sank. That could only mean one thing: Sean hadn't returned. He was still with Brid.

Marie studied her. "Sean probably will be back any minute."

Ruth forced a smile she didn't feel. "Oh, I'm sure."

"But I'll lock up just in case."

"Of course. Good night, Marie."

"Good night, Ruth."

Ruth tried to be optimistic. Marie was probably right. He'd be back soon.

RAIN SPLASHING against the windows woke Ruth the following morning. She sat up at the table, where she'd been asleep with her head on her folded arms. She stretched, her neck stiff. Through sleepy eyes, she looked around Sean's kitchen and everything came back to her in a rush. She'd been waiting for Sean to return. Swallowing hard, she pushed the chair back and stood up. The kitchen light was still on and she flipped off the switch.

She was starting to come to the realization that Sean had never returned. She made her way down the hall to Sean's bedroom. The door was open and the bed made. Her heart sank. The speculation of the pubgoers seemed to be true: Sean was back with Brid.

"Right, then," Ruth whispered to herself.

Shaking, she headed to her room. Multiple strands of thoughts wound themselves around the inside of her head. But the predominant thought was that Sean was no longer available. It was a blow she had not anticipated. At least not seriously. She knew she couldn't stay there anymore. There'd be no way she could share space with him, knowing he was with someone else. Her heart actually hurt.

She laid her suitcase on the bed and opened it,

then began to remove her clothes from the bureau and threw them in. Hangers clattered along the metal rail as she hastily removed her dresses from the wardrobe. Once packed, she texted Nicole, telling her she'd be in Dublin by late morning and she'd explain when she got there. Then, using the landline, she called for a taxi. She filled an envelope with the money she owed Sean, and then wrote his name on the front of the envelope and set it against the sugar bowl on the kitchen table. Finally, she fed the dog and gave him a pat on his head.

She wrestled her suitcase down the staircase and watched out one of the windows for her taxi, praying that Sean wouldn't arrive first.

Five minutes later, when the taxi pulled up, Ruth pulled on her raincoat and, taking one last look to make sure she had her purse, carry-on, and suitcase, she exited the pub, closing the door and locking it behind her.

As the cab drove away, she did not look back.

SEAN GROANED and opened his eyes. He'd fallen asleep in the chair by the hearth in Mackie's kitchen. The fire had long gone out, and cold ashes in the grate greeted him. The letter he'd written to Ruth was tucked beside him in the chair.

He glanced at the clock on the wall and was surprised at the time. He'd been up until four, writing and rewriting his letter to Ruth.

He pulled on his coat and decided to check on the orchard before heading back home. It didn't bother him that it was raining. After a quick visual inspection, he jumped into his car and started it up.

The village was quiet, and the only car he passed on the way was a taxi. The pub was shrouded in darkness, and none of the drapes in the upstairs rooms had been opened. He wondered if Ruth was still sleeping. He whistled as he pulled onto the paved asphalt in front of the pub. He had a good feeling about the day. His only plan was to give Ruth his letter and take it from there. There was going to be no more holding back.

After he unlocked the front door, he flipped on the lights for the pub's interior. Still whistling, he took the stairs two at a time, anxious to see Ruth. At the top, he frowned. It seemed unusually quiet.

"Ruth?" he called out.

When there was no response, he called out again and headed down the hallway to her room. The door was wide open, the bed made, and the room devoid of her personal belongings.

Swallowing hard, he trotted down the hall to the kitchen. Shep stood up to greet him and absent-mindedly, he reached out and patted the dog. Glancing around the kitchen, his eyes landed on the envelope leaning against the sugar bowl.

It felt as if everything inside of Sean emptied out.

"Ruth," he whispered. Reluctantly, he picked up the envelope and tore it open. Pulling the sheet of paper out, he noticed the euro notes inside. He sighed. He read her letter and then he reread it. She had written that it was time for her to leave and she was meeting up with Nicole in Dublin. She thanked him for all his help and had signed it, "Ruth Davenport."

Sean fell into the chair, crushed. He couldn't believe that she had left. Just like that. He couldn't understand why she would leave without saying goodbye to him personally. He wanted to kick himself for going to Mackie's the previous night. He should have come right home.

Suddenly, he groaned as he realized that he had left with Brid and then not returned all night.

"You stupid eejit!" he muttered with force. He had no one but himself to blame for Ruth's departure. What on earth was she supposed to think with him being out all night?

He stood up. He had to right this somehow. Before she left Ireland, Ruth Davenport had to know how he felt about her.

He knew she was returning to America that week. But he wasn't sure of the day. And he couldn't guarantee that she hadn't changed her ticket.

"Damn!" he muttered. He folded the envelope that contained his letter for Ruth, tucked it in his pocket, grabbed his coat and keys, and headed out the door.

# CHAPTER TWENTY-TWO

Ruth paid the cab driver and she and Nicole stepped out at the Departures terminal of Shannon airport. The driver pulled their suitcases and carry-ons from the trunk of his car and set them down with a thump on the sidewalk.

Once she'd caught up with Nicole in Dublin, they'd spent the remainder of their four days sightseeing. At first, Nicole was disappointed to hear that it hadn't worked out with Sean. And it was all Ruth could do to prevent her sister from returning to Ballybeg to have a "talk" with him. Their days had been jam-packed. They rose early and didn't return to their hotel until very late at night. Ruth did not want to have any spare time to think about Sean.

She did not want to go home. She did not want to leave Ireland, but there was no reason for her to stay, and that depressed her more than anything. She had all the material she needed for her book, but her heart wasn't in that, either. Forget about romance; she might just write a tearjerker.

"Are you all right?" Nicole asked quietly by her side. Her sister had been solicitous over the last few days without being overbearing. Ruth was glad she was there.

Ruth nodded. "I am." She gave her younger sister a reassuring smile that she didn't feel and said, "It's time to go home. Let's check in."

There weren't that many flight desks to check out from at the small Shannon airport, and that suited Ruth just fine. As she walked toward the desk, towing her luggage and carry-on behind her, something in her periphery caught her attention. Looking right, she blinked when she saw Sean walking toward her. She froze to the spot, unsure what to do. If she was smart, she'd run to the check-in desk and get her boarding pass. As Sean approached her, she noticed two things about him that were missing: his grin and his toothpick. Dark smudges circled his eyes, and he was in desperate need of a shave.

Ruth remained rooted to the spot. She told herself to remain firm, no matter what he tried to sell her. Nicole looked at her, wondering why she had stopped. Following her sister's line of vision, she spotted Sean and said, "Look, I'll head over to check in."

When he finally reached her, Ruth asked, "How did you know I'd be here?"

He looked sheepish, and he scuffed the toe of his shoe along the industrial linoleum. "I didn't, actually. I knew you were leaving this week, so I've been showing up at the airport every day, hoping to see you before you left."

"What day is this?"

"This is day number four," he said. He looked tired.

"You've been coming here every day for the last four days, hoping to run into me?" she asked in disbelief.

He nodded.

"What time do you get here?" she asked. She was trying to reconcile her impression of Sean with these actual events.

"I get here when it opens up in the morning, and I don't leave until the last plane for America has departed," he said.

Ruth was speechless for a moment. "I don't know what to say."

He shuffled his feet some more and looked down at them as if they held all the answers of the universe. This was a different Sean. There were no wisecracks, no grins, no teasing, no toothpick. This was Sean, anxious and vulnerable.

Ruth bit her lip.

"When I came home, you were gone," he said quietly.

"I felt I'd be in the way between you and Brid."

He sighed. "I know how it looks. I left with her and didn't come home until the following morning."

"The locals were practically placing bets as to whether the two of you were getting back together."

"And is that what you thought?" he asked.

"Yes," she said. "You have history, and it seemed natural that the two of you should reconcile."

"Natural to everyone but me," Sean said. He stood with his fist on one hip. "Ruth, I don't love her anymore."

"Oh," was all she could muster. She was a master at written dialogue, but this was all she could come up with. She dared not hope. Not again.

"When I left with Brid, I told her that I didn't love her anymore, that I had moved on. Then I drove her home," he said.

Ruth stiffened.

"And after I dropped her off, I went to Mackie's house to think about things. Mainly you." He pulled an envelope from inside his jacket pocket and thrust it into her hands. "Take this. This is a letter from me, trying to explain how I feel. I spent the night writing this. Then I fell asleep." His weary eyes were pleading. "This is me. When you get back home, sit down and read it."

She looked at the envelope, noting Sean's familiar scrawl. "Thank you."

"No. Thank you, Ruth," he said. Hands in his pockets, he walked away, shoulders hunched.

Ruth stood there for a moment, watching him disappear out the doors that led to the parking lot. She wondered if she should go after him, but she was afraid.

Nicole came back to Ruth and looked around. "I'm all checked in. Where'd Sean go?"

"He left," Ruth whispered, still looking at the doors he'd departed through.

"He left? What did he want?"

"To give me this," Ruth said, holding up the envelope.

Nicole raised her eyebrows. "Oh. Aren't you going to read it?"

"I will, once I check my bag and get my

boarding pass," Ruth said, not fully registering yet her encounter with Sean. "He's been coming here every day for the last four days, hoping to run into me to give me this letter."

She reached for the handle on her suitcase but Nicole took it from her. "No, Ruth, you're not doing a thing until you sit down and read that letter."

"He told me to go home and read it," she said, feeling detached.

Nicole shook her head. "Come on, there's seats over by the Arrivals gate."

She led Ruth over to the bank of seats and said, "I'm going to grab a coffee. Do you want one?" She parked their carry-ons and Ruth's suitcase by Ruth's feet.

Ruth shook her head and sat down.

She crossed her legs, opened the envelope, and slid out its contents. Carefully, as if it were a priceless antiquity, she unfolded it.

*My darling Ruth,*

Ruth clutched her hand to her chest and pressed her lips together.

*B*EFORE YOU SHOWED *up on my doorstep that night six weeks ago, I never thought I'd open my heart again to another woman. I'd told myself that I would never put myself in a position to be hurt again. I've worked very hard at this over the last few years. And yet you, in a few short weeks, have undone everything. I think I have been in love with you since I opened the door and saw you standing there, drenched and muddied.*

*There are so many things I've grown to love about you that I don't know where to start. But let's start with your name. Ruth. It's biblical. Epic. I love your red hair, and I'd give my kingdom to run my fingers through it. I love your green eyes because I see every shade of Ireland in them. I love every frock you wear, and I have never loved flowers more because of them. I love your laugh. I love your optimism and hope. I love how I feel when I am with you, like everything good and wonderful is possible.*

*If I could have my way, I would spend the rest of my life loving you. I want you next to me in the car as we explore, together, this beautiful country. I want to look up and see you there, smiling. Then I would know all was right with the world. I want to learn how to bake, just so I can have the desserts on hand that you love so much. I want to be the man who zips up your dresses in the morning and then unzips them at night. I want to kiss every inch of those scars on your legs. I want to put a jar at the foot of the bed on the damp, rainy nights so you'll never be cold. I want to grow old with you, sitting next to the fire with a hot cup of tea and talking about everything from the weather to the outrageous price of petrol at the pumps to who we're going to root for in the All-Ireland final.*

*With you, I had hoped for a happily ever after. I love you and would gladly be hurt for you a thousand times over, without even having to think about it.*

*I will never stop loving you.*

*Sean*

RUTH REREAD the letter several times, tears falling freely. She was aware of the curious stares from fellow travelers, but she didn't care. She tucked Sean's letter carefully into her purse, then pulled out a tissue and wiped her eyes. All sorts of thoughts raced through her mind. She looked around for Nicole and saw that she was deep in conversation with a handsome man at the coffee counter. It was another ten minutes before she returned, coffee cup in hand. "Well?"

Ruth stood up, and in a shaky voice said, "Well, it looks like I'm staying."

Mindful of her coffee cup, Nicole hugged her and said, "Yes! Now go on. I'll be fine."

Nicole walked Ruth back outside and flagged a taxi for her. They stood on the curb with Ruth's luggage at their feet. They hugged and cried and said goodbye.

"I'm so happy for you, Ruth," Nicole said. "Nobody deserves this more."

That made Ruth cry harder.

SEAN WIPED down the counter of the bar. It was quiet, just a few locals. That was all right with him; he wasn't in the mood anyway. He'd been back from the airport for almost an hour. He unfolded the paper on the bar and began to read the sports section, but he couldn't concentrate.

The door opened from outside, but whoever had come in just stood there. Sean was about to shout out to close the door because of the draft coming in when he looked up and saw Ruth with her luggage, standing in the doorway with the afternoon sun streaming in around her. He froze.

*She came back.*

Forgetting about the paper, he slipped out from behind the bar and in a couple of strides was in front of her.

"I'm looking for accommodation," she said softly, her eyes searching his face.

With a grin, he asked, "For how long?"

She smiled and said, "For the rest of our lives."

Speechless, he pulled her to him, lifting her in his embrace so that she had to look down at him. She cupped her hands around his face, and without a word, laid the sweetest kiss on his lips.

Hungry for more, he gently set her down and pressed her against the wall. His heart pounding, he kissed her with lips that were warm and insistent. She yielded to him, and he was relieved.

Reluctantly, he pulled away, but only because he needed to catch his breath. He just couldn't believe she was standing there in front of him. It was like the best Christmas morning ever. Protectively, he put his arm up on the doorframe to shield her from the nosy pub patrons. Although they appeared only semi-conscious half the time, they'd break their necks tripping over each other to get out of the pub and tell everyone the news.

With his back to the interior of the room, he smiled down at her. The way she looked up at him—he'd be able to live on that look alone.

Feeling a bit bolder, a bit more sure of himself, he reached out and ran his hand down the side of her face. It was even softer than it looked, if that was possible.

"Come here, darlin'." She came willingly into his embrace. He wrapped his arms around her, and closed his eyes when he felt her slide her arms around his waist.

He kissed the top of her head and whispered, "Welcome back, Ruth."

# EPILOGUE

SEAN LOOKED around the brand-new kitchen and made sure all the ingredients were gathered on the countertop. He'd been out earlier in the orchard with the boys, inspecting the apple trees on his daily rounds. The blossoms looked good, and he thought it was going to be a good year.

He'd inherited the house and the land from Mackie. There had been a small bit of money, and it had been divided equally among him and his brothers. With Ruth's encouragement, Sean had finally realized his dream of becoming a grower. He was in the middle of a ten-year contract with Bulmers, and also supplied apples to SuperValu. But it was Ruth who had wisely pointed out that the pub was an integral part of village life, so he'd sold it to Calvin and Marie, and the business had continued. He did not miss the late nights or the pub in general.

In the last twelve months, while Ruth had been on bedrest for her most recent pregnancy, he had remodeled the kitchen with the help of his brothers. It had been gutted and rebuilt from the ground up. They were going through the house, one room at a time. The original bathroom had been remodeled and another one added to accommodate their growing brood.

He looked at the eager young faces gathered around the kitchen island. The three boys, Charlie, Billy, and Johnnie, who was only three and who insisted on helping just as much as his big brothers, were seated on stools, lined up like the steps of a staircase. The baby, their only daughter, was in her high chair, eating biscuits and making a mess like she usually did. He regarded her adoringly. With her red hair and green eyes, she was the image of her mother.

Sean clapped his hands. "All right now, today's Mammy's birthday, and we're going to make her a lovely cake." He bent over his phone to find the recipe he had saved.

"Boys don't make cakes!" said his oldest, Charlie, still with some mud on his face from his hurling match earlier that morning.

Sean straightened up. "Says who? Of course they do. They make cakes and they do the laundry and they change the nappies—"

"Not Ruby's stinky ones," said Billy, the second oldest at five and already a rogue, who broke into a fit of laughing.

"Now, there's no making fun of the baby," Sean admonished in a mock scold.

"Ah, she's a girl!" Charlie said in disgust.

"Yes, she is, but have I ever told you how wonderful girls are?" Sean asked. The two older ones looked up at him with suspicion. "Why sure, isn't your mammy a girl? Think about that."

"Mammy's a girl?" Billy asked in surprise.

"Well, she's not a boy," Sean pointed out.

"I thought she was just a mammy."

He looked at them, his heart bursting with pride, and said, "Are we going to stand around all day talking and complaining, or are we going to get this cake made?"

At that moment, Ruth entered the kitchen. Sean's features softened at the sight of the love of his life. Her color was finally starting to return. The last pregnancy had been difficult since day one, and he eyed baby Ruby suspiciously with one raised eyebrow, wondering if it was a premonition of things to come. But Ruth was starting to get some of her old form back. There were fine lines around her eyes, but their sparkle hadn't dimmed.

"What's going on in here?" Ruth asked, beaming. She tousled the hair of the older boys.

"We're baking you a birthday cake," Billy answered.

Johnnie automatically raised his arms and whined, "Mammy."

"Is it my birthday?" she asked, feigning surprise and looking up and winking at Sean. She pulled Johnnie up into her arms and balanced him on her hip. He was a mama's boy and there was nothing that was going to be done about that.

"It is," answered Billy. "How old are you, Mammy?"

"How old do you think I am?" she asked.

The five-year-old looked thoughtful for a moment. "Are you nine?"

"That's very close," she said.

Ruth stepped over to Sean and leaned into him for a kiss, and he was only too happy to oblige.

"Would you be the mastermind behind all of this?" she asked her husband.

"I've been sworn to secrecy," he said, kissing

her again, always liking the taste and feel of her. Never tiring of it. The four kids were the proof of that.

"Can I help?" she asked, surveying the scene.

"No, now shoo," Sean said, giving her bum a playful swat with the dishtowel.

"All right then," she said. With Johnnie on her hip, she bent over to the baby and asked, "How are you, gorgeous?" Ruby cooed and smiled in response.

Sean stood back for a minute, surveying the scene. He studied the faces of his wife and children, reveling in his own happily ever after.

## ALSO BY MICHELE BROUDER

**The Escape to Ireland Series**

Her Fake Irish Husband

Her Irish Inheritance

A Match for the Matchmaker

Home, Sweet Irish Home

**The Happy Holiday Series**

A Whyte Christmas

This Christmas

A Wish for Christmas

One Kiss for Christmas

A Wedding for Christmas

**Soul Saver Series**

*Claire Daly: Reluctant Soul Saver Claire*

*Daly: Marked for Collection*

Visit my website and sign up for my newsletter at www.michelebrouder.com to get news about future installments of the *Escape to Ireland* series as well as other releases.

# ABOUT THE AUTHOR

Michele Brouder is originally from the Buffalo, New York area. She has lived in the southwest of Ireland since 2006, except for a two-year stint in Florida. She makes her home with her husband, two boys, and a dog named Rover. Her go to place is, was, and will always be the beach. Any beach. Any weather.

CPSIA information can be obtained
at www.ICGtesting.com
Printed in the USA
BVHW030940091221
623627BV00001B/44